THE STRAW HALTER

Betsy is eighteen years old when she is sold in the market-place to farmer Daniel Forrester. Since childhood her beauty has sparked jealousy from many quarters, and unlike many in her position, she has been taught to read and write. Although Daniel does not treat Betsy like a servant as her first husband did, his jealousy when a young man comes to work on the farm is extremely disruptive. Betsy decides to investigate the death of her father who reputedly died when she was a baby. Will she discover the truth about her ancestry and her relationship with the farmhand?

THE STRAW HALTER

THE STRAW HALTER

by

Joan M. Moules

Magna Large Print Books
Long Preston, North Yorkshire,
BD23 4ND, England.

British Library Cataloguing in Publication Data.

Moules, Joan M.
    The straw halter.

    A catalogue record of this book is
    available from the British Library

    ISBN   978-0-7505-2946-4

First published in Great Britain in 2007 by Robert Hale Ltd.

Cover illustration © Nigel Chamberlain by arrangement with Alison Eldred

Published in Large Print 2008 by arrangement with
Robert Hale Limited

Magna Large Print is an imprint of Library Magna Books Ltd.

Printed and bound in Great Britain by
T.J. (International) Ltd., Cornwall, PL28 8RW

For Marion and Henry
With Love

Chapter 1

MARCH 1820

Betsy stood proudly, her dark hair gleaming with vitality, her deep-blue eyes searching the faces as they moved along. All around her the bustle of the fair went on, stall-holders calling their wares, and the smell and movement of cattle only a few yards away from where she waited with the man who was about to sell her. The pungent smell of sausages cooking drifted across to where they were standing and she wondered whether by the evening she would be cooking a meal for a man as yet unknown to her.

Betsy knew she was beautiful and intelligent above her station. She knew also that a farmer looked for practical skills more than physical attributes in a wife and, in spite of her confident bearing, she was worried.

She could cook, milk, churn butter and cream as well as any of those alongside her, who sagged, heads down, in a manner suggesting compliance and unquestioning obedience to their husband and master.

Yet she could see it in the men's eyes as she boldly stared them out. They were impressed, but they never paused, never asked whether she was of any use to a farmer beyond satisfying his sexual needs, and he could do that outside of a wife. Those buying today wanted above all else a woman who would work, do her duty about raising a family and…

The man who stood in front of her now was short, his square-jawed chin giving him a fierce and determined look, but his eyes betrayed a slight hesitation. He stood looking for a few seconds and she lowered her own gaze. She knew she was too arrogant. The husband who was selling her had repeatedly told her so.

'I am the master. I give the orders. You obey.'

He wasn't selling her because she was lazy, but because she had failed to give him the son he craved.

'You're barren,' he taunted her, 'a beautiful, barren bitch.'

The farmer turned to the girl standing next to her – a soft, blue-eyed, rosy-cheeked lass who looked much too young to become a wife, but had the rounded sturdiness that indicated she could work all the hours that were needed, and produce a line of sons to till the land. There was a murmur of voices and when Betsy looked up the thickset prospective buyer had moved on and another was now gazing at her. He grinned, and she was sure he winked, then he too went further along the line where half a dozen others waited while the men standing near them talked and laughed together.

Some day, said the voice inside her, the voice that always seemed to land her in trouble, some day this will be like a bad dream. Women will be men's partners, they will share, they will not be sold like cattle in the market-place and at the fairs. Betsy knew that most of the others with her there today accepted their fate, but she never had.

Given in marriage to George Hatton three years ago when she was fifteen, she had rebelled from the start.

'I'm not like the others, I've learnt things,' she told him. 'I want to be a helpmeet not a servant.'

George, startled, had replied, 'You will be a good wife. You will work on the farm, in the kitchen, and you will bear my sons and daughters. If you do well there'll be no complaints, you're a comely-looking wench and I'll take pleasure in you.'

Now he was selling her, the ultimate humiliation in her eyes. Tears threatened and she blinked hard, gazing downwards as the others were, but for a different reason. She would not let them see her tears, for they might attribute them wrongly.

The stern-looking man was back, and now

he stepped closer and spoke to her. 'What be your name then?'

His voice was out of keeping with his appearance. It wasn't harsh, as his face was. His voice and his eyes, which were looking at her intently now, were almost gentle.

'Betsy – sir.'

'Can you milk and bake?'

'Yes.'

'And make butter and cheese?'

She nodded her head.

'Answer in the proper manner.'

'Yes.' This time there was a long pause before she added very, very softly, 'sir.'

She saw the glimmer of a smile in his eyes and her interest was aroused. This man was different from most of them. He didn't shout because she wasn't as servile as the rest. In fact he seemed amused.

Betsy felt her temper rising. She had no desire to amuse either. She stared him out and had the satisfaction of seeing him move on again.

George Hatton, standing behind her leaned over and said, 'Behave yourself. If you come back with me you'll pay for this.'

Ten minutes, ten humiliating minutes later, as other men gave her the eye, and made lewd suggestions, but didn't buy, he was back. She had watched many being led away, happy in the knowledge they would have a roof over their heads and food in their bellies for the next six months at least, and longer if they gave satisfaction in every direction. She knew she was being foolish with her stubborn daring. Why couldn't she be as subservient as most of the girls here today? What was it that drove her to antagonize every man who looked?

She knew the answer of course, but seemed incapable of suppressing the angry pride inside herself, the pride that told her she was man's equal. The farmer was speaking to her again and so engrossed was she in her own thoughts she hadn't realized.

'Pardon, sir?' she said.

'I asked if you were healthy?'

Her chin rose defiantly, dark-blue eyes sparked with anger and as the husband who was selling her started to answer she said, 'Of course. I would not stand here in the market if it were otherwise. I am not a cheat.'

She watched a dark shadow pass over the prospective buyer's face, saw his knuckles showing strain in his clenched fists, and knew that once again her unruly tongue and quick temper had worked against her. Yet he did not move but continued to gaze at her, the expression on his thickset features unfathomable.

He reached for her hands and inspected them thoroughly. This time she did not obey her natural instinct to pull them away, but allowed them to be ruthlessly scrutinized.

Abruptly he let them go. 'I'll take you,' he said.

She felt a quick surge of jubilation. For he had said the words to her and not to the man who was selling her, and was even now standing with the halter at the ready. Wasn't this proof that you need not be totally without voice? His face and bearing were ungainly, he was a deal older than she was, yet there was something in his manner that told her he would be a good and fair master. While he conducted the business of buying her she lifted her head high and smiled broadly at everyone who looked, men, women and children alike.

Her happiness was short-lived however, when he slipped the straw halter around her neck and prepared to lead her away.

'I will come without that.'

'It is right,' he answered, 'it proves I have bought you and not stolen you.'

'It makes me as a beast in the field, and the Bible says man has dominion over the fish of the sea, over the fowl of the air, and over the cattle...'

'But you are a woman, not a man. Woman was made from Man's rib.'

'I–'

'I am, however, happy to see that you know your Bible. We shall read some tonight after we have eaten. Come now, for I can see you would not wish me to carry you off.

And when we are out of sight of the market I will take the halter from your neck.'

Betsy was silent. Better surely to go along with this than to fight him here. She saw that her man must be left his pride – he would be a brave one indeed to go against tradition. She knew without doubt that if she made a fuss he would sling her over his shoulder and carry her away like a dead beast.

She allowed herself to be led out of the market, and when she had scrambled on to the farm cart which was with the others in the yard, he checked his horse then climbed into the driving-seat and they set off. Her fingers closed round the device circling her neck, yet instinct told her to bide her time. Less than a quarter of a mile along the dusty track he reined the horse in and came round to the back of the cart.

'Here,' he said roughly, 'lean forward.' With gentle fingers he lifted the halter from her neck. 'It is only made of straw,' he said quietly, 'hardly worth making such a fuss about. It will take us an hour to be home, are you comfortable, Betsy?'

'Yes, thank you.'

'Don't you wish to know my name?'

She inclined her head and this gesture, as it had back there in the market place, seemed to rouse him to anger.

'Answer when you are spoken to.'

'Yes.'

'It is Daniel. Does that make you think of anything from your Bible?'

Wonderingly she gazed at him. 'He was thrown to the lions but God shut the lions' mouths and they did not hurt him.'

'And I will not hurt you, Betsy.' Reaching further into the cart he pulled her forward and his lips touched hers, softly at first, then harder and harder, with a hungry passion. Then with one swift movement he was in the cart, his hands fumbling with the petticoats beneath her skirt.

Betsy pushed him away with all her might, and saw the amazement and anger in his eyes even as he fell to the ground. The horse, frightened by the commotion, suddenly took off and Betsy scrambled to the front of the cart where she grabbed the reins, managing to bring him to a stop several yards along the dusty lane. She talked soothingly to the beast and when she glanced round saw that her new husband was brushing himself down. Then he strode to the cart, anger in every movement, grabbed the reins from her and set off at such a pace that she clung to the side in her desperation not to be tipped out. After a while he slowed the pace but it was well under the hour when they reached the farmhouse. Betsy found it the most frightening ride of her life.

'Go inside and look around while I see to the horse,' Daniel said when they reached

16

the farmhouse. It was the first time he had spoken to her since the tumble from the cart and she felt both relief and apprehension at the sound of his voice. Her mother had warned her often enough about her quick temper, 'Watch it girl,' she used to say, 'or it will get you into trouble.'

Daniel had the right to do what he would now. She would grow used to it, but that sudden onslaught had taken her by surprise. He was no better than the rest of them in spite of that gentle voice. He unlocked the door, then moved away without looking directly at her, and as she stepped over the threshold she felt a tremendous fear about the future with this man.

Her three years with George Hatton had been hard. She had discovered how mean he was, and how single-minded. But at least he hadn't paraded her round the market at the end of a rope as some did, before standing her in the line of wives for sale, and for that she felt grateful. She had told Daniel she wasn't a cheat but he only asked about her freedom from disease, and she spoke the truth. He had not mentioned fertility and the main reason George Hatton had sold her was because she had not conceived, in spite of his persistence. Would this be the same, night after night, often several times, in a desperate effort to have a son?

She moved further into the farmhouse

kitchen and looked around her. Suddenly desperately tired she pulled a wooden chair from beneath the table and sat down. Resting her arms on the table she thought about the evening and night ahead and said a silent prayer that her new husband would leave her alone for a few hours at least. A resigned feeling came over her as she relived those moments on the road when she had fought him. No doubt she would suffer for that. A dry sob escaped her lips and she nestled her face into her arms to stifle it. Daniel found her like that ten minutes or so later when he returned. At first he thought she had collapsed, but when he bent over her he realized she was asleep. A strange expression flitted across his face as he gazed at her. She stirred and looked up.

'I'm – sorry. I must have fallen asleep,' she said, embarrassed that he should discover her like this.

'I'm not surprised, it has been a long day. Stay there and I will fetch you a drink, then we shall talk.' He wasn't asking, he was telling her, and although her instinct was to busy herself with these tasks now, she sat on and listened to the domestic sounds around her. When he placed two tankards of ale on the table and pulled out another chair to sit beside her she turned to face him, very conscious of their physical nearness to each other.

'Do not be afraid of me, Betsy. I have a temper, as you seem to have also. Nothing wrong in that. I – I should have waited until we reached Redwood and I now regret that I did not, but, although I am years older than you, I am a man with passionate blood in my veins and you set it racing as never before.'

Abruptly he pushed his chair back and stood up, 'Now drink up, then I will show you round the place. I'll take mine in the other room where I have things to attend to.'

Betsy knew she had aroused him again and when he had gone she took several deep breaths, then sipped the ale he had brought to her. It was stronger than she was used to. In a short while he returned and took her over the farmhouse.

They went upstairs first. There was a main bedroom which housed a double bed, a sturdy dark wooden wardrobe, an equally dark chest of drawers and a marble wash-stand containing a jug and basin. Another smaller room was furnished with a single bed and smaller chest and a chair. Down-stairs next to the kitchen was a room with a large desk, a heavy dining-table, four chairs upholstered in green and two brown leather armchairs. The curtains were of heavy velvet, again in dark brown and the whole effect was depressing. 'Well that's it, Betsy. Come, I'll show you the farm while it is still light.'

'The closet is here,' he said, indicating a small shed in the garden, 'I will wait if you wish to relieve yourself.' She shook her head and they continued on the tour. 'The well is over here and the dairy there.' He waved his hand in the general direction. 'Mixed farming, cows, sheep, and crops. The shepherd lives in his own cottage and Jim the farmhand lives along the lane and comes in every day. Redwood is a small farm, but we have a busy life and there will be plenty for you to do, mostly in the house and dairy but outside on the farm too if I need you there.'

Back in the kitchen Daniel said, 'I promised we would read from the Bible this evening. But first we will eat. I usually have bread, cheese and pickle at this time. Tomorrow you can take over this aspect of our life. I will give you a list of food I enjoy, and if you wish to add to this we can discuss the matter.' She nodded, grateful that she did not have to prepare a meal while he was hovering. Tomorrow while he was working outside she could look around and plan her routine.

'I will also give you some money for housekeeping and I shall expect you to account for how it is spent, at least at first,' he said. 'We are not rich, but with careful management we can get by comfortably.'

They sat at the scrubbed wooden table to eat and she discovered to her surprise that she was very hungry. Afterwards she washed the plates and mugs in the bucket of water standing outside the back door before they went into the sitting-room, 'because there are two comfortable chairs in there and only one in here,' he said. 'On my own I prefer the kitchen.'

He went to a bookcase in the corner and returned with a Bible. Without consulting her he read from St Matthew, 'Therefore whosoever heareth these sayings of mine and doeth them I will liken him unto a wise man, which built his house upon a rock...'

As Daniel closed the Bible he smiled across the space between them. 'I understand you read; perhaps you would like to do so one evening. Meanwhile tell me more about yourself. All I know is that you are eighteen years old and breathtakingly beautiful. I want to know much more.'

'I'm the youngest of eight children. My father died when I was a baby and I don't remember him at all.'

She paused and Daniel said gently, 'Your mother – is she still alive?'

'Yes.'

'Then you must introduce us later. She will want to know you are well cared for.'

'I can take care of myself. I've been doing so for years.'

He looked at her sharply, 'Have you quarrelled with her?'

'That is my affair. You may have bought a wife, but you haven't bought her soul as well as her body.'

She glanced across to where the straw halter now hung on a nail behind the door, then looked quickly away. His expression changed and in an instant the atmosphere became charged with tension. He clenched his hands until the knuckles looked brutal, then suddenly he said, 'That's fair comment, I suppose. However, if we are to live together in some sort of harmony, and I hope we are, then you must learn as I must learn. You are far too quick to jump. I have no wish for you to be *too* subservient but I expect a certain–'

At that moment there was a terrific hammering on the door. Daniel looked startled, but was up and out of the room faster than she would have thought possible. She heard anxious voices, both men's, one of them her new husband's. After what seemed a long time to her, sitting apprehensively in the armchair, Daniel returned.

'I have to go out, trouble at Denmeads, Martin there, is our nearest neighbour,' he told her. 'I don't know when I'll be back, so if you are tired get yourself to bed and I'll be along later.' He hesitated for a second and she thought he was going to kiss her, then he grimaced and said, 'Tonight of all nights, but maybe I won't be long. You'll be all right, the back door is locked and I'll take my key. Don't push the bolts though.' Then he was gone and she heard him talking to whoever it was in the hallway, imagined him pulling on his boots to go and help with whatever catastrophe had befallen his neighbour.

Alone in the farmhouse Betsy wasn't sure what she wanted to do. It was only half past eight, far too early for bed. Nevertheless she went upstairs to their bedroom and un-packed her clothes, placing them neatly in the drawers and wardrobe space that Daniel had indicated would be hers. She drew the curtains, leaving a two-inch gap so the room would catch the first light of dawn, then she went downstairs and looked at the books on the shelf from which Daniel had taken the Bible earlier. Several were farming manuals but there was some fiction. She took one of these, returned to the armchair and began to read. It was a story about a servant-girl and when the lady of the house was men-tioned Betsy closed her eyes, remembering her own days with the lady of the house where she had been sent to work when she was ten years old.

Mrs Wallasey had been kind to her from the beginning, asking about her brothers and sisters, sending little treats home with her on the few occasions when she was able to go. These were usually on Mothering Sunday and Christmas Day if she was lucky, although she actually found it better to be at the big house on Christmas Day rather than with her own family. This did sometimes make her feel guilty.

She had started work in the kitchen at Wren Court and for three months had not seen anything of the rest of the house, except the back stairs leading to the bedroom that she shared with two other girls. They were both older than she was; one was twelve and one fourteen, and they resented having such a young girl with them. At night Betsy was so tired she simply wanted to sleep, but they talked and giggled, mostly about the butcher's boy who delivered the meat for the house every day.

Jane, the older one, tripped her deliberately on more than one occasion, both in the kitchen and upstairs in their tiny attic bedroom. She thought about that room now and realized that she had never had a space to herself. Before she went into service she slept with her siblings, girls at the top and boys at the bottom of the bed. Then she shared with the two other girls at Wren Court. Jane, the fourteen-year-old, was bossy and spiteful and never tripped her when anyone else could see what she was doing. It was always done slyly and Betsy quickly learned to watch out for this.

Most times she managed to stay on her feet and no real damage was achieved, but one day, when she had a pile of dinner-plates in her hands, taking them from the cupboard over to the stove, she didn't see Jane's foot come out and she went sprawling across the floor, while the plates clattered around her.

Cook, standing by the stove and with her back to what was going on in other parts of the kitchen, turned quickly. Hauling Betsy to her feet she said, 'You are getting so clumsy, child, this is the third time this week you've skidded across here like that. How many of those plates are broken? Because it will have to come out of your wages at the end of the year.'

Betsy set about picking up the plates. Miraculously only one had broken, although another was chipped. 'They weren't the best set, Mrs Bates,' Betsy said, while out of the corner of her eye she saw Jane watching her. The older girl quickly turned away and busied herself chopping onions on the long wooden table, while Annie, who always followed where Jane led, kept her eyes on the mixture she was stirring at the other end of the table.

'Tut, tut, girl, get a move on,' cook said sharply, 'and make sure you pick every piece up. Then wash them all and check for cracks or chips.'

Betsy swallowed the words she almost said, for cook would never believe Jane had tripped her up on purpose, and Annie would stick up for her friend, then she herself would be in more trouble for telling tales.

Both girls kept out of her way for the rest of the morning, not even looking in her direction, and her temper rose by the hour. Why were they nasty to her? Because she was young and they thought they could get away with it? Well, she'd show them. She would trip Jane up and deny it when the girl tried to blame her, as she knew she would. The thought of revenge for all the nastiness she had endured in the last few weeks at Jane's hands made her glow with excitement.

Cook harried her for the rest of the day, but she managed to keep her temper, remembering her mother's words when she had started here: *Watch that tongue of yours girl, because if you lose your place you can't come back here, I've enough mouths to feed as it is.*

That was another strange thing, she'd always been the skivvy at home, none of the others seemed to do as much as she did. Out of five brothers and two sisters she was the only one who had had to leave home so early to earn a living. Her two sisters were grown up, they were the eldest of the family, yet Betsy always had the feeling that even when they were young children they never had the sort of treatment she received, but of course she couldn't know for sure. As for the boys, they were expected to bring in wood for the fire, but very little else.

She closed the book on her lap and let her memories flood her mind. Betsy wondered what her own life would have been like if *her* lady of the house hadn't died when she had. She had been sent to see her after the plate-crashing incident and she wasn't nearly as terrifying as cook had led her to believe. She had a gentle voice for a start, and her questioning was not harsh.

'Cook tells me you tripped with a pile of plates in your hand and broke some,' she said. 'Well, these things do happen from time to time. Perhaps you were carrying more than you could properly manage. Was that it?'

Betsy hesitated, then, 'No, ma'am,' she said. Mrs Wallasey was silent for a moment and Betsy thought she was going to lose her job. Instead her lady said softly, 'Cook also tells me this is not the first time. That you often skid across the kitchen floor. Perhaps you should try to make two journeys instead of one and maybe even be a little slower, Betsy.'

Now, all these years later, Betsy thought it was the use of her name that had triggered the tears then, for even her mother scarcely used it, and cook referred to her as *girl* or *you girl*. Whatever the reason she could not stop her eyes from filling and the tears overflowing and running down her cheeks. Mrs Wallasey came closer and touched her hand. 'It's all right, Betsy, nothing is going to happen to you. Just be more careful in future, there's a good girl.'

A week after that encounter Mrs Wallasey sent for her again. 'How are you getting on here, Betsy?' she said.

It wasn't in Betsy's nature to pretend, and after a moment's hesitation she answered truthfully, 'I do my best, ma'am. I don't seem to please.'

Gently Mrs Wallasey had lifted Betsy's hands from her side and examined them. They were red and tender, raw with continually washing the kitchen floor, peeling great bowls of potatoes, and generally doing all the tasks the other two no longer did. She remembered how ashamed of them she had been, and as she tried to wriggle them out of Mrs Wallasey's firm grip her employer said quietly, 'Do Jane and Annie share the heavier and dirtier tasks with you, Betsy?'

She remembered, even now, how she could not look her special lady in the eyes and not tell the truth. Instead she had concentrated her gaze towards the floor and said, 'We all do as cook tells us, ma'am.'

She had felt a very soft finger beneath her chin, gently easing her face upwards. 'I'm glad to hear that. You may go now, Betsy.

You're a good girl.' She was out of the room before the tears fell and had wiped them away well before she was down the back stairs and in the kitchen.

'Well,' cook said, 'what did Mrs Wallasey want with you?'

'To – ask how I was getting on with the work, Mrs Bates.'

'And what did you tell her?' Cook's huge body loomed over her.

'All right,' she lied.

'Good. Come on now, you've wasted enough time when you should have been working, so get and help Annie with those vegetables. I hope milady isn't going to make a habit of asking the scullery-maids how they're getting on. Hmmph.' She bustled over to the kitchen range.

A week later cook told her that Mrs Wallasey was short of a maid upstairs and that Betsy was being sent up for the time being. She was ten and a half and had worked at Wren Court for three months.

The same noise that she had heard earlier quickly brought her back to the present and this time she stood up, the book still in her hand, to check what it was. For a couple of seconds all was quiet, and then it came again, a scratching noise by the window. Nervously Betsy walked across the room. The brown curtains were drawn and yet someone was out there – there it was again, a rattle against the window as though someone was trying to open it. She put her hand on the curtain. Should she pull it and see? Whoever it was couldn't get in that way and Daniel had warned her that the doors were all locked. She wished he was there with her now.

Deciding to ignore the noise she returned to the fire and picked up the heavy poker from the hearth. If whoever it was did manage to get in she would at least have something to defend herself with. The silence as she sat in the chair again was eerie. She knew she could not concentrate on the book, and she didn't want to wander around the place. The candles gave out a soft glow, but enough for whoever was out there to know the room was occupied. Maybe they had seen Daniel go off and knew she was here alone. The noise began again; it wasn't a tap, nor yet a knock, more of a scraping sound. Suddenly she knew she had to see who was there. They were, after all, on the other side of the glass at present.

Armed with the poker she returned to the window and although her free hand was trembling she pulled the curtain back with a flourish. She didn't know who was the more surprised, she or the large black cat balancing on the wide sill and hammering to be let in. She unlatched the window and stood aside as the animal jumped through. It walked across to the fireplace and began to wash itself.

'My goodness, puss, you gave me a fright,' she said. The cat ignored her and continued its ablutions. Bending to stroke it she said, 'You obviously live here, so I hope we'll be friends. I'm Betsy by the way. Reckon Daniel will tell me your name when he gets back.' As she straightened up she caught sight of the straw halter hanging on a hook near the door and a grim feeling came over her.

'I'd best leave it for now, puss, but it's got to go,' she murmured, 'I can't have it staring at me every time I look over there.'

It was tempting to take it down, destroy it now, but something warned her she shouldn't. Yet Daniel had taken it off once they had been clear of the market, even if he had hung it there as a symbol.

Biting her lip she turned away and returned to her chair. She seemed to hear Mrs Wallasey's voice in her head: *Betsy, have patience and many of the things you want will happen. It must be done gradually, you simply cannot change such ingrained traditions and customs overnight. But your time will come child, and you must be prepared for it.*

To this end Mrs Wallasey had taught her to read and write, lent her books, and talked about so many subjects. They discussed

31

politics and the King while Betsy made herself a new apron from material bought in the market. They talked about the latest fashions while she sewed ribbons on to Mrs Wallasey's new but rather plain hat, and sometimes they mulled over the sermon the minister had preached in church. Mrs Wallasey had been in her usual pew, and Betsy at the back with the other servants, but it didn't stop them talking together about what had been said.

'Well, it was meant for all of us, Betsy, "you in your place and me in mine,"' was her lady's comment once when she was shy about this. And Betsy didn't mind the business of high and low places. It seemed fair. Mrs Wallasey and her family had money and land and could afford to hire people to do the things poorer folk had to do for themselves. This was right and proper. If she, Betsy, one day had money and land, she too would do this she felt sure. No, there was nothing wrong about having a place in life, but it should be a movable place.

It had been a wonderful four years and she had loved her employer dearly. She had still slept in the attic room with Jane and Annie, but they were wary of her and no longer played tricks or tried to get her into trouble. In any case she saw little of them except late at night and early in the morning and her mind was too full of the wonders of learning to give either of them much attention. Once Jane said, 'What do you do up there all day?'

'I sew, mend, run errands...' She did not tell them that when Mrs Wallasey went for her meal she always left her a book to read, or an essay to write. 'You have a good brain, Betsy, don't let it rust,' she had told her.

'I was eager for it, puss,' she said to the cat, who had finished cleaning himself and was lying in front of the fire. 'I saw the other side of life when my lady was alive. She took me with her to so many grand places and she taught me so much. You have no idea.'

The cat looked up then, its green eyes glittering like the emeralds her special lady often wore. Betsy settled herself once more in the armchair and picked up the book, but within ten minutes she was asleep and the book had slipped down the side of the chair. She didn't even wake when Daniel returned at almost midnight. He saw the flickering candlelight in the sitting-room and was startled to find his wife sound asleep in the chair.

Chapter 2

A gentle kiss on her forehead woke Betsy. She stirred in the chair, and then looked up, startled to see Daniel gazing at her.

'Time for bed I think,' he said, holding his hand out to help her up.

'Is it all right – whatever the trouble was?' she asked.

'Yes. Two cows in difficulty calving. Martin saw to one and I took the other, but it was a long haul. Bad luck to get two of 'em in trouble at the same time.'

'You – you didn't lose any?' she said.

'No. Now he has three healthy calves. Twins, that's unusual, and where most of the trouble was, and a single.'

Betsy stood up, 'I'm so glad. You must be tired. I'll fetch you a drink and something to eat.'

'Just a drink, Betsy. There's some cider in the pantry.'

As she moved away he said quietly, 'And Betsy I'll make no demands on you tonight. I've had a long day and I'm tired. We'll simply lie together.'

He was asleep long before she was, and as she lay listening to his regular breathing she returned in her mind to those earlier years she had been thinking about during the evening, and to her previous husband, George Hatton, whom she married when she was fifteen. If Mrs Wallasey hadn't died and her son and his wife taken over the house who could tell how different her life might have been. She had always been wary of John Wallasey when he visited his mother and took pains to ensure she was never alone with him. When he inherited the property and came to live there with his wife whom, he said, would need a maid, life became nasty. From dodging his wandering hands whenever he could catch her alone, to putting up with his arrogant and overpowering wife, Betsy went from one extreme of working conditions to the opposite. She had determined to go to the next mop fair and seek work in a kitchen again when matters were taken out of her hands.

The new 'my lady', it seemed, was not ignorant of the ways of her husband and within six months of taking over she had found Betsy a spouse. George Hatton was nearly thirty years old and had taken over one of his father's farms. He needed a wife and Sarah Wallasey decided she needed an older and plainer maid.

'I have spoken to your mother,' she told Betsy, 'and she is in complete agreement. We will give you a small dowry and you will wed George Hatton next month.'

Betsy had wondered at the time why they should give her a dowry but there was no time to ponder the question. It was three months before the mop fair would come, and short of running away and trying to fend for herself she had no choice. Her mother would not take her back; she had been only too glad to push her into service, and how long would she last with neither food nor money? It would be foolish to try.

Much later when she thought about the situation calmly she came to believe that the older Mrs Wallasey had made some sort of provision for her and it was this that her son and his wife gave her in the form of a dowry. She was sure that that had not been the intention of the lady she regarded as her special guardian angel but there was nothing she could do about it.

George Hatton had one overwhelming ambition. To have a son. 'Or two or three,' he told her. To that end they retired in the early evening and if sheer persistence could have worked, he would have been a happy man. Betsy came to dread the nights, and was thankful they were both so busy on the farm and in the house during the day. His desire dominated his life and she never conceived. Would the man sleeping deeply by her side now be the same? As he moved she felt his arm brush against her and she held her breath, but he did not wake. She closed her own eyes and thanked the Lord for one night of respite.

When Betsy woke the next morning she was alone in the bed, but she could hear sounds from the kitchen. She poured some water from the jug into the large china bowl on the washstand, washed, dressed and went downstairs. Daniel was sitting at the scrubbed wooden table eating egg and bacon and a hunk of bread. 'Sleep all right,' he said.

She almost nodded, then remembered the effect this had on him, and said, 'yes thank you, Daniel.'

The cat came and rubbed against her legs. 'You are a beauty,' she said, bending to stroke its sleek glossy back.

'Dumbo seems to have taken to you, he is not always so friendly.'

'Dumbo?' she queried.

'Because he's dumb. Can't make a sound although he does open his mouth and try sometimes. He lets you know what he wants just the same.' Daniel glanced down at the animal. 'Makes a heck of a racket with his paws when he wants to be let in.'

'Yes, he does, he really startled me last evening while you were out. I thought some-one was trying to burgle the place.'

Daniel scraped back his chair. 'I'm off. I'll be in about noon with Jim who helps out on

37

the farm. We'll have some bread and cheese and you can cook a meal for you and me this evening. There's a larder full of ingredients.'

'Yes.'

He turned at the door. 'You're so beautiful, Betsy, whatever was he thinking about to sell you?' Then he was gone.

They came together that night. Daniel was gentle at first, nothing like he had been in the cart on the way back from market. As he caressed her and she responded their lovemaking became more passionate until, exhausted they went to sleep in each other's arms.

Her days fell into a pattern of working, often in the dairy with Hannah, the pretty little fourteen-year-old, cooking and shopping in the market in nearby Lampney. She went in once a week with Daniel when he took his milk and butter to be sold.

Most evenings were spent reading and talking with Daniel after their meal. She learned that he had been to school when he was a boy and worked on his mother's farm before he began in the mornings and when he came home again. She thought he seemed a natural scholar and, had he been born into a wealthier station in life would surely have gone to university. They had some lively discussions and went up to their bedroom happy and stimulated.

Most nights they made love at least once and for the first time since she lost her virginity Betsy knew the ecstasy that was possible with a man.

It amazed her in those first weeks how deeply contented she was with this man, who had, after all, bought her in the marketplace. The work did not bother her at all. She had been used to it since she was old enough to toddle but her awakening feelings for Daniel did surprise her. She was discovering so many things about her new husband. She learned quickly that his temper was powerful but slow to ignite and to her surprise she found she wanted so much to please him.

The halter was there still, evidence of something she felt to be degrading, yet she had not asked him to move it.

One morning when he was out on the farm and she was sweeping the kitchen she paused beneath the straw halter. She reached up and unhooked it from the nail. If I burnt it would he notice it wasn't here? she thought, and knew immediately that he would. The idea was swiftly followed by her strong feelings that he too had to recognize the place women should have in the world. She knew the humiliation of being 'bought' and he had to acknowledge and do something about the situation.

She had thought this when she was with

George Hatton too. He had not bought her as Daniel had, but he treated her as a servant nevertheless. On the occasions, near the beginning of their marriage, when she had defied him and tried to make him understand her feelings he had hit her.

'You are my wife and you will do as I say,' had been flung at her many times. He was mean with his money too, and there was never any chance that she could leave and find employment anywhere else.

During that first month with Daniel she had learnt to trust him as a human being. He was blunt and lacking in some of the finesse she had absorbed when she was with Mrs Wallasey, but she could not blame him for this. She realized how fortunate she was to have had those years and Daniel at least treated her mind as equal to his. Carefully she replaced the straw halter.

'One day,' she said to Dumbo, who was following her around, 'one day he will understand how shameful that is.'

Betsy and Daniel had been together for six weeks when Daniel's brother arrived. It was midday and, along with Jim the cowman, they were sitting round the kitchen table eating. Sometimes when they were very busy they took their food into the fields with them, but most days they came to the farmhouse kitchen. Jim was tall, skinny and very quiet, except when he was with the cows; he talked to them all the while. 'Has a way with cows, has Jim,' Daniel said to Betsy one evening. 'Understands 'em more than he does humans. That's one reason why they give us so much milk – they'll give to Jim they will.' Betsy had become used to the silent young man sitting down to eat with them. Although he didn't appear to, he actually ate his meal quickly and was always finished first. Pushing his chair back, he'd say, 'I'll get back then,' and glide silently through the door. On this particular day they had only just begun their repast when there was a banging on the door and a fair-haired man dressed in breeches and check shirt came in.

'Joseph, what brings you here?' Then, turning to Betsy he said, 'This is my brother Joseph.'

Joseph's eyes blatantly admired her and he moved along the backs of the chairs until he was immediately behind her. 'Heard my brother had wed but didn't know he'd found such a beauty. You must come over to Sandilands Farm and meet the rest of the family. Ma'll be surprised.'

Daniel stood up and pushed his chair back from the table. 'Will you eat with us, Joseph, then state your business here. We've a deal of work to do.'

'That's OK, Dan. You and Jim get back to

work, I'll entertain your wife and yes, something to eat and drink would be great. I rode over and it's thirsty work.' Daniel walked to the dresser and returned with a plate and an earthenware mug. He cut a hunk of bread, a thick wedge of cheese and poured cider into the mug. 'Sit yourself here,' he said sharply, indicating his place, 'I'll take the stool over by Betsy.' He came round with a kitchen stool and placed it next to her, moving his plate of food across.

Throughout the meal she was very conscious of Joseph watching her from across the table. He was as unlike Daniel as if they were not related. Daniel hadn't mentioned family to her until she said to him one evening, 'How many brothers and sisters have you, Daniel?'

'Only the one, and t'isn't often we see each other.' Then he had changed the subject. Now, though, he raised his voice, 'So what brings you over here, Joseph? Is Ma well?'

'Same as usual. Best bring Betsy over to see her.' Jim finished his meal, and with a nod to Daniel, slid through the door.

'*He* doesn't say much,' Joseph observed. 'So, when you coming over?'

'Very anxious to see me suddenly, aren't you? You've never bothered before.'

'Ma likes to know what you're up to.'

'When it suits her,' Daniel said. Then, turning to his wife, 'Come on, Betsy, we've

42

work to do outside. Leave this for now.' He turned to his brother as he left and urging Betsy in front of him, said, 'Tell Ma we'll be over one day.' Outside he took hold of Betsy's hand saying, 'Don't look so surprised. Didn't think I would leave you in there with him, did you?'

'I can take care of myself you know, Daniel.'

There was half a smile on his lips and in his eyes as he said, 'Maybe you can, yes, I daresay you can do so very well, but I'm taking no chances. I know my brother and he's not laying his dirty paws on you, Betsy.'

Joseph came out to them. 'Always the un-sociable creature – you don't change much, Dan.' Turning to Betsy he said, 'When you need a bit of fun get him to bring you over to see us. It's not much for a beauty like you stuck in this dismal place.'

Before she had time to reply Daniel said, 'You help Jim with the cows, Betsy, while I find out what my brother wants from us. I won't be long.' Then, taking Joseph's arm, but not in a friendly way, more like a man of law taking a prisoner, he ushered his brother back towards the house.

True to his word, Daniel wasn't long, no more than fifteen minutes, and he looked to be in a black mood. She said nothing in front of Jim, but later in the house when they were eating the supper she had prepared she said, 'So, did you find out what your brother wanted, Daniel?'

'I did. He wanted to see you, the news that I had taken a wife had reached them. He also wanted to borrow money. Joseph is always broke. Ma usually bails him out but I gather this time she said no.'

'He lives with your Ma?'

'Yes. Manages the farm, but he's a poor farmer. I *will* take you over one day when it suits m – us.' Betsy's spirits rose. He almost said, *when it suits me,* then changed it to *to when it suits us* and she felt a glow of achievement. In the weeks of their marriage she had seen Daniel change from giving her orders to discussing things with her. He listened to her views, and they talked everything over together. He had a surprising turn of humour which delighted her. She thought it would be interesting to meet his mother and see what her farm was like.

'Joseph hasn't a wife then?' she said.

'No.'

Joseph had looked about thirty to her, but realizing that her husband was not in a mood to expand on this subject, she swiftly changed it. Later, in bed he said, 'Betsy, did you think Joseph was handsome?'

The question took her by surprise. 'Not really,' she said. His arm came round her, 'Oh Betsy, you're so beautiful, beautiful inside as well as outside, I love you very much.

Our marriage is good for you too, isn't it?'

'You know it is. I am happy, Daniel and – and I love you too.' Their lips met in a passionate kiss, and as she guided him into her, she gave herself with an abandonment she had not even suspected she was capable of before knowing him.

Nothing further was said about visiting Daniel's mother and in any case they were busy on the farm. She mentioned his brother one evening when they were having their meal. 'Did you and your brother grow up on Sandilands Farm, Daniel?' Smiling, she added, 'I'm trying to picture you as a boy.'

'I was an ugly little boy.'

She laughed. 'How do you know? No one came over to you and said, "You are an ugly little boy," did they?'

Suddenly there was an uncanny silence, she could hear no sounds at all, not even her own breathing. Daniel broke it with a single word which came out as almost a sob.

'Yes,' he said.

He looked so vulnerable sitting opposite her, his head bowed and very still, almost as if he were afraid to move. She rose swiftly, went across and put her arms round his shoulders in a big hug.

'Who, Daniel, who said that to you? Joseph?'

His head sunk lower on to his chest and she could feel him trembling. 'No, not

Joseph. My mother.' As she laid her cheek against his she tasted the salty dampness of his tears.

Betsy knew she was pregnant the morning after she conceived. No sooner had her feet touched the ground than she had to rush for the slop-bucket. The sickness left her feeling weak, and she went back to sit on the bed for a few minutes to recover. Her thoughts flew to what they had eaten for supper last night. Pork, vegetables and a thick gravy. This had never given her any problems before.

She still felt decidedly queasy and slowly made her way downstairs to empty the bucket. Daniel would be in for his breakfast soon. The very thought of preparing food made her heave again, and it was then that she realized she was with child.

A surge of joy filled her being. She loved Daniel and wanted his child, but also there was the thought deep within her that she was safe. After all the years of abuse with George Hatton which had made her dread the physical side of marriage and, at times, had almost broken her spirit, she was overwhelmed with shock that she could, after all, conceive.

Not that Daniel had expressed a need for a family above all other considerations, yet, somehow, it still made her feel good. It would surely please him, and more and more Betsy wanted to please her husband. Slowly she ran her hands over her stomach. She would nurture their child, was even now doing so, would feel it move within her, would suckle it, play and teach it even as Mrs Wallasey had taught her in those wonderful years when she was working at Wren Court. A child, a baby, she thought, how will Daniel react?

He would be pleased, of course he would, even though he had such a different attitude to her first husband. He would want a baby and they could afford it. In those first months of marriage to Daniel she had had a firm grip on their financial affairs.

'You are an unusual woman, Betsy,' he said to her once.

'Unusual. I don't understand what you mean Daniel.'

'Most women wouldn't have any idea about finance and certainly would not become involved in the money side of the farm.'

'I'm not most women, I'm me. I can reason and work things out as well as you can. As most women would be able to given the right chances.'

'There's no need to bristle like that, I agree with you, my love. It's the rest of the world you have to convince.'

'I suppose so. But how, Daniel? When women are bartered for in the market-

47

place,' her gaze went towards the door where the straw halter hung, the one symbol her husband refused to relinquish. During the time they had been together they had grown closer than she would have believed possible, yet that necklace of straw was always there, reminding her of her status.

'It will come,' he'd said then, 'to the ones who want it. Many who have known nothing else simply accept their place but you have seen a different way of life and have learnt so much. The answer is to educate everybody, regardless of gender, so that each person has an equal chance in life.' He walked over and put his arm round her shoulder, 'There will always be some who are leaders and some who are led. You are strong, like my mother, she too is a strong woman.'

'She doesn't approve of me.'

'That makes us even more of a pair,' he said quietly, 'because she doesn't approve of me either.'

'Why do you think that, Daniel?'

He shrugged dismissively, 'Because she has never liked me. I was the odd one always. She doted on Joseph when he was born, she treated my cousins from over the hill with more affection than she ever showed to me. I have often wondered why she hated me so much.'

'I've only seen her once I know, dear, but

I don't think she hates you. She–'

'Leave it,' he said suddenly. 'I don't want to talk about it, about any of them.'

Now, with the knowledge of a child of her own she wondered again about Daniel's family. His mother, fair like her younger son, Joseph, had hardly made her feel welcome the day they went to Sandilands Farm. She was plump, with piercing blue eyes and a rather coarse skin, and Betsy could see that once she had probably been pretty. Now, after she had spent years out in all weathers, the elements had taken their toll. She had given them thick chunks of home-made bread with cheese, but conversation had been stilted. Betsy knew she had not contributed much herself and Daniel had seemed almost surly.

His mother had issued instructions to Joseph about what to buy when he went to market next day but had practically ignored her and Daniel. Betsy wondered whether his mother knew that he had bought her, and an embarrassed flush filled her cheeks even now, at the thought of it.

But that was in the past. She had had no choice then, although she had tried to escape from George Hatton on the journey to market. It had been a weak attempt, she realized, for how would she have fared with no money or food and no prospect of work until the next hiring-fair? She had felt so angry when she knew he was selling her; it still simmered within her, yet it had turned out so well. Daniel was as unlike George as it was possible to be. He discussed things with her. About the farm, the house, the country...

As she set the breakfast things out her thoughts returned to her single visit to Daniel's family and she wondered afresh why his mother seemed to dislike him so much. For although she had said the opposite to Daniel to try to reassure him, she knew he spoke the truth. She sensed it very strongly in the atmosphere. She also knew that Joseph, like his brother, could read and write, but after meeting the boys' mother Betsy doubted if she could. Perhaps that was why she was so disagreeable, because Joseph would surely have told her that Daniel's wife was not illiterate. Was she jealous? Did she feel inferior? Mentally Betsy shook herself. This wouldn't do, she had work to get through, and the lovely thought which she was holding close to herself, that she was with child brought a happiness to her heart. This evening, when they sat down after their meal she would tell Daniel, because she knew without waiting for further proof that she was pregnant.

By suppertime Betsy had changed her mind about revealing her condition too soon.

Even though she was sure she was carrying Daniel's child it might be best to wait a week or two at least. She hugged the knowledge to herself for the rest of the evening, but next morning when she rose she had to dash for the bucket again. Fortunately Daniel was already downstairs, but on the third day he came up for something he had forgotten and caught her on her knees over the receptacle.

'Betsy, what is it, my darling?' When he saw what was happening he gently rubbed her back and once it was over helped her up. 'You are ill.' In spite of the deep concern in his voice her mind flew back to his question at the market, *Are you healthy?* and her angry reply brought a flush to Daniel's cheeks.

'Of course I'm not. Having a baby isn't an illness, it's a perfectly natural state.' She regretted her outburst immediately. It was not how she had wanted to tell him the news.

'I'm sorry,' her voice caught on a sob, 'I meant to tell you properly, not like this.'

He caught her to him. 'It's all right, there's nothing to worry about Betsy. Women have babies all the time and everything will be fine. You are pleased, aren't you?'

Torn between frustration that he should think she was worried about giving birth, and what she now recognized as genuine

51

concern when he had thought she really was ill, she tried to laugh, but it came out as a little sob and as he stroked her hair and held her close she was powerless to stop the tears gushing from her eyes.

'Oh Daniel, I'm being so stupid and weak.' She moved from the circle of his arm. 'I'm sorry, I was going to tell you once I was certain. I am certain. Do you want a child, Daniel?'

'Of course I do. Do you?'

'Yes, oh yes.' His arms engulfed her once more and his strong workworn hands stroked her hair tenderly.

The sickness went on for two months, but once that early-morning stint was over she insisted on doing everything the same as before. Daniel wouldn't allow her to do anything that involved lifting or moving even the lightest of loads, and she was glad that he was out on the farm for most of the day, for she feared her temper would flare if he became too protective.

She sang as she worked about the house and in the dairy and began to think about names for the baby. Not after either of their parents, but perhaps Daniel for a boy and Elizabeth for a girl. She shivered with the warmth of feeling this baby was engendering in her and the pleasure she anticipated in discussing it all with Daniel.

Three months into her pregnancy she miscarried. Daniel insisted on fetching the village midwife to her in spite of her protests that 'It's too late, she can do nothing now that I cannot do for myself.'

It took Betsy a long time to recover. She alternated between tears and temper. 'I've never been a cry-baby,' she said to Daniel after one particularly bad spell, 'so why am I now?' Yet whenever he offered comfort she turned on him until he too lost his temper.

One night he said, 'The most important thing is that you are all right. I thought I was going to lose you, Betsy, and I don't think I could bear that.'

'But I lost the baby. It was your baby too but you don't seem to care about it now.'

'Of course I do, but you are more important to me than all the babies in the world. Betsy, it's so long since you loved me...' But she turned away.

Betsy was amazed at how devastated she felt over losing her unborn child. Sometimes her misery was so great she didn't know what to do with herself. If Daniel was gentle with her she turned on him for acting stupidly and if he was tough she turned on him too, accusing him of not caring about anything but his own comfort. She knew she was being totally unfair and this added to the guilt she felt, because although she had proved she could conceive, she hadn't been able to carry to full term. She slept badly and longed for the comfort of the old days at Wren Court and her special lady. She could have talked to her about this and maybe it would have helped.

Before Mrs Wallasey died they had discussed so many situations and problems. 'There is usually an answer to most of our troubles,' she remembered Mrs Wallasey saying once, 'although sometimes it isn't the one we seek. Mostly you just have to get through as best you can, Betsy. Women are stronger in that respect than men I think.'

Betsy clung to the memory. She *was* strong, she was strong enough to overcome this setback but she needed time. Time to get the hurt out of her system, and although she loved her husband dearly now, part of her shied from him and she retreated more and more into herself, refusing to go to market on the pretext of things to do in the house and dairy.

When Daniel suggested they should pay a visit to her mother Betsy shook her head.

'Why, my darling, why?'

'Because she doesn't care about me, never has. I've managed all these years without her and I don't need her now.'

'But she's family, Betsy, your own family. When we do have a family of our own I would want them to visit us.'

She turned away sharply. 'We haven't a

family, we lost our baby, or don't you remember?'

Without moving nearer he said softly, 'I will never forget, but one day we will have children together Betsy.'

She remained silent, trying to stem the trembling that had begun inside her. Then she turned and ran from the room. That night he climbed silently into bed beside her, not touching, not even giving her the perfunctory kiss which he had been doing in spite of her coldness.

She lay awake for hours, long after he had turned over on his side and gone to sleep. She felt guilty because she knew she was behaving badly, yet seemed powerless to stop. She didn't realize that she was crying until a great sob shook her body and she turned her head into the pillow to stifle the sound. Suddenly she felt Daniel's arms cradling her and heard his voice murmuring endearments.

'I'm no use, Daniel. I can't even have our child.'

'Of course you can, my dearest. God has His reasons and that one wasn't meant to be. I still need you desperately.'

'Oh Daniel. I never thought I could feel like this. I'm as weak and vulnerable as any woman.' As she buried her face against his chest she didn't see the laughter in his eyes.

'You – weak! Never. You are going to show

the world that women are as good as men – and I shall help you do so, never fear.'

Jim, the farm-hand, lived alone in a tiny cottage down the lane from the farm. This had once belonged to his widowed aunt with whom he lived until she died. He went home at the end of each day, but when Thomas Shooter came to the farm seeking work during haymaking Daniel let him sleep in the loft above the stable. He was tall, fair-skinned and blue-eyed but there was an arrogance in his manner that Betsy found irritating beyond words. Not that he was anything but polite to her for the brief time he was in the kitchen. For Daniel's sake, because he needed the extra help badly for a few weeks, she kept silent but she was not unaware of the way he ogled her while pretending not to. It revived memories of why she had been married off to George Hatton when she was fifteen. This new farm-hand was no better than her old master had been and she felt relief that he was temporary and that once haymaking and harvest was finished he would be on his way.

She came from the dairy one morning and found him standing against the wall outside. He seemed to be leaning on the wall for support.

'Tom, what's the matter. Are you all right?'

For a moment he didn't answer, then he

looked at her, and for a second she saw the gleam in his eyes and backed away.

'I'm bad,' he said, 'feeling rotten. Master sent me back to rest.' Instinctively she reached towards him, then she said quietly, 'Too much sun. Best get to bed for an hour. You'll be fine by morning.'

'Reckon so.' His eyes held hers for a moment. 'I'll be on duty tomorrow,' he said, and his voice faltered slightly. She turned from him and went across the yard, then she heard a strangled sort of cry and looking back saw him slumped by the wall of the dairy.

All wariness gone she hurried back and helped him up. With her arm supporting him, he walked into the kitchen. She pulled a chair out from beneath the table and eased him into it. He rested his head on the table. She went to the larder for the earthenware pitcher of water she kept on the stone floor after drawing it from the well earlier. She dipped a beaker into it and hurried over to him.

'Here, sip this.'

'You're very kind, missus.' When she didn't reply he said quietly, 'I'd best get over to my bed afore I faint again.' Her natural instinct was to help him, support him, yet there was something not quite right here. His voice sounds weak she thought, but his eyes ... what was it she saw there, not frailness certainly, more like excitement.

'Yes,' she said, adding, 'I'll send some food over for you later.' He went slowly, as though every step was an effort, and she watched through the window until he was out of sight round the corner by the stable. There was no one around to send with food so she took him some bread and cheese after she had set their own meal on the table. She climbed the steps to the loft, laid the plate on the top one and tapped the door. Then she hurried away because she had recognized the look he had given earlier and it took her right back to the market-place and the men's lustful eyes as they assessed her. She was back in the kitchen before Daniel and Jim came in for their meal. Later that afternoon she mentioned the incident to Daniel.

'Yes, he came over queer. I sent him back to the stable to rest. He didn't come here, did he?'

'I saw him and took some bread and cheese over just before we had ours.'

'Was he all right?'

'Don't know. I thought he'd be resting so I left it on the step outside.'

'No use to us unless he can work,' Daniel said. 'I'll check on him before I go over to the field in a moment.'

He kissed her tenderly before returning to work. Was it her imagination, she thought, as she worked in the dairy during the afternoon. Or had she seen that look in this particular farm-hand's eye, the look which said *you are a beautiful woman and I want you.* Had he feigned illness to get her alone in the kitchen?

Tom appeared on the farm the following morning ready for work. He came into the kitchen midday with Jim and tackled his bread and cheese with gusto. Jim rose silently as usual at the end of the meal and returned to his beloved cows. Tom lingered until Daniel said, 'Get moving then, there's work to be done out there.' He left for the fields himself soon after and Betsy began clearing the crocks from the table.

A few days later when Betsy was working around the house she heard a noise downstairs in the kitchen. Daniel always called out. 'It's only me, Betsy,' if he returned to the farmhouse during the day, but this time there was no such greeting. She came downstairs to find Tom standing by the scrubbed wooden table, his hand casually resting on the back of a chair. Her thoughts flew to Daniel: had there been an accident?

'Tom, what's up?' Her voice was sharp with anxiety and when he didn't answer but simply looked at her a tremor passed over her body. 'Mr Forrester – is he all right, what's happened, Tom, tell me.'

She was half-way out of the door when she heard him behind her. 'He's all right,' he said, ''Tis me. I come over queer again. Need some water.'

'Go and sit down while I fetch it.' She was trembling as she moved towards the larder and he stood perfectly still watching her.

'Go and sit by the table,' she said again, warning bells ringing throughout her being. She intended to wait until he had moved before filling the mug she took from the shelf, but he suddenly clutched his chest and staggered in her direction. Grabbing hold of her he murmured, 'I'm so dizzy...'

As she dragged him towards the chair she was conscious of his closeness, she could feel his breath coming in short little gasps and wished Daniel was around to help. Suppose he died on her. She had never had anything to do with death and illness and this was the second time in a week that this lad had been stricken. They reached the chair and she practically pushed him on to it. He clung to her, moaning softly, and as she tried to move his grip tightened and he pulled her closer until their faces were almost touching. One of his hands slid down her thigh and began pressing her to him. Jerking herself away sharply she delivered a stinging slap to Tom's face.

'Get yourself back to the stable this minute,' she said. He went without another word. She was still flushed with anger nearly an hour later when she was preparing the evening repast. If they were not so short-handed she would tell Daniel about it and she knew Tom would be through the door faster than a shaft of lightning. But they had to gather the corn before the weather broke and they *needed* the extra pair of hands. Another couple of weeks and all would be harvested. Surely she could avoid being alone with Thomas Shooter for that short time. In any case she could defend herself against the lustings of men like Tom.

She knew now why the girls in the kitchen at her first place had been so mean with her, but at the time she had not fully understood. They were jealous because the master never looked at them. Why did she have this devastating effect on the male sex?

She had thought her husband hard-featured and less than handsome when she first saw him, yet now she noticed his strong bone-structure and not his swarthiness. She knew his tenderness as well as his temper and, strangest of all, she loved him. She enjoyed their lovemaking and her greatest wish was to have his child or children. A spasm of sadness passed through her as she wondered yet again if this would one day happen.

Twice now she had miscarried. Daniel hadn't known about the second one because it was such early days and he was at market when she had this tremendous pain and struggled to the closet outside. She went to bed for a while afterwards to regain some strength but in spite of slapping her cheeks in an effort to put some colour back to them Daniel had said when she placed his meal in front of him that evening, 'Are you well, Betsy? You look tired, my love.'

Smiling, she assured him she was fine and began to ask about the market and whom he had met and talked to there.

It had been frightening for her and she felt awful for days afterwards, but she was glad Daniel had not known. When things settled down maybe she would try to find out why this was happening to her. Perhaps she should speak to her mother, as Daniel wanted, but for a reason different from his. Maybe she could tell her if it was something that ran in the family, whether anything had happened to her when she was a baby to prevent her carrying her own babies to full term.

A slight noise outside shot her mind back to her present problem, but it was only Dumbo tapping at the window to come in. She let the cat inside, fed him, then went to the bedroom to wipe a cool cloth over her burning cheeks before Daniel came home for his tea.

She had no further trouble with Thomas Shooter during the next few days. If anything he seemed to ignore her presence, except for a brief 'Thanks' when she put his food on the table at midday. The harvest was nearly finished now and soon he would be on his way. She felt sure his dizziness had been put on and she shuddered as she realized the implications it could have. However she was glad she had said nothing to Daniel about the young farm-hand's advances. He was young, strong and apparently a good worker. Nevertheless she would be glad to see the back of him.

The harvest supper was fun to prepare, enabling Betsy to meet some of the other farmers' wives, and she was looking forward to the evening, not least because Tom Shooter would be on his way the following day.

Betsy noticed Tom watching her from across the long trestle-tables set up in the barn at Redwood for the traditional supper, and she refused to catch his eye. She stayed close to Daniel for most of the time, but inevitably they became separated as people moved around afterwards. It was then that Tom crept up behind her.

'Missus,' he said quietly, 'can I talk to you for a moment, it's very important.' She swung round to face him.

'Go on then.'

'There's far too much din in here, I can't shout this out. 'Twill take two moments only. If we just step outside–'

'No. If you have anything to say do so here.'

'All right. But you won't like it. This will be better said in private.'

'Have your say and be done with it,' she said, 'then we can get on and enjoy ourselves.'

'That's what it's about, enjoying yourself. It can't be much with him, your husband,' he spat the word out with contempt, 'he'll take anything female and you are too beautiful for that. What did he do, buy you in the market-place?' Her hand seemed to move of its own volition as she slapped his face, leaving a red stinging patch on his cheek. Then she walked away. She was trembling so much, with anger and humiliation – she knew not which was the dominating feeling – that she quickly escaped to the door and stood there for a few moments, fighting for control. She dared not risk going outside for he would surely follow her and in his present mood he was strong enough to overpower her easily.

The throng moved around her, laughing, happy, full of food and drink and the knowledge that it had been a good season and the harvest was in. Amazingly, no one seemed to have noticed the little encounter and Tom had quickly taken himself off.

After a time she returned to the centre of the room and helped in the clearing away.

Then she joined in the dancing and merriment, but part of her felt dead. This should have been a joyous celebration, but for her, now, it was an ordeal to be got through.

She took the last of the crockery across the yard back to the farm kitchen while Daniel saw off the rest of the revellers as they made their way back to their own places. When she heard a noise behind her, she whipped round and saw Tom emerging from the pantry. In two strides he was there, beside her, both hands gripping her shoulders and marching her into the spacious shelved pantry, he kicked the door closed.

'No one treats Thomas Shooter like that,' he muttered as his hands went up her skirt, 'I'll have you, my lady, one way or another.' She beat her fists against his chest and his hands slid from her garment as he fought her off and tried to restrain her. But she was frantic and as he eventually managed to grip her hands and hold her at arm's length it gave her the chance to distance herself sufficiently to lift her leg and aim for his groin. With a cry of pain he abruptly let go and Betsy wrenched open the door and fled, leaving him doubled over and groaning in agony.

She longed for Daniel to come and take her to the safety of their home. Yet as she ran back to the barn the thought came to her that Daniel would kill him if he ever found out what he had tried to do. She knew Tom was staying one more night in the loft over the stables, but thank heaven he would be leaving now that the harvest was over. Best surely to say nothing to her husband.

After breakfast the following morning Tom said to Daniel, 'I'll come by next year at harvest time,' then, looking directly at her, 'Goodbye, missus. Thanks for everything.' His hand touched her thigh as he slipped past.

When she went over to the dairy fifteen minutes later he was hovering near the wall. In the far distance she saw her husband walking towards them. Tom obviously saw him too, for he moved away.

'You'll pay for this,' he muttered as he drew near to her, and without stopping walked off down the lane.

Chapter 3

For a few days after Thomas Shooter left Redwood farm Betsy was jumpy. There had been something almost sinister about the lad. Fair-skinned, clean-looking, oozing with freshness and vitality and yet... His words about making her pay for her rejection of him kept coming into her mind, but what could he do? He had left the farm now, left the area and was on his way to new adventures and new women.

She shuddered and thought once again how wonderfully things had worked for her. The best thing that could have happened was when George Hatton sold her to Daniel. She was still filled with shame that such a thing should happen to her or any woman, but she knew that in her case it had led to such happiness.

She was totally in love with her husband now. A year ago she would not have thought it possible to love a man so much that she was willing to let go some of the ideas she felt passionate about.

She was often surprised by her husband's patience because he had a temper that erupted like a volcano sometimes, but she noticed it was mostly when he was convinced someone or something was completely wrong. He had tremendous patience with the animals and a calmness when he was amongst them or working on the land he loved.

Daniel had taught her so much about many things too. He had a good mind and as a boy had attended the village school regularly, whereas she had almost no learning until Mrs Wallasey took her in hand. But he admitted to her that he had no ideas of fine living, and she had because she had witnessed and been part of it in her first employment.

'Oh Daniel, that doesn't matter. What matters is being together, working for what we believe in.'

'That women will one day rule the world,' he said affectionately. They were sitting together on the old settee and his arm was round her shoulders.

'Only if they have the intellect to do it. Then they should have the chance alongside men. Mrs Wallasey used to say...' she hesitated and his laughter rang out.

'Go on, then, tell me what this wonderful person used to say.'

'Now you're laughing at me. It's fine for you, men have had it their way for so long, but men and women were born with a brain, some greater than others, and it should be used. In the Bible it says we must use our talents and we all have them.'

He pulled her towards him, 'I'm not laughing at you, my darling. But you must admit that most of those wenches standing in the market with you had very little brain.'

'It isn't their fault, they've had no chance.'

'Maybe, maybe. But you are different. You are special, Betsy. You have something many do not have and it isn't just intellect.'

She moved slightly and turned to face him. 'Beauty can be a curse,' she said.

'Yes, you are beautiful, but that wasn't

what I meant. I sometimes wonder...' he broke off in mid-sentence.

'What do you wonder, Daniel?' Her tone was gentle.

'How it is you love me, ugly little Danny boy.'

'Is that what *she* used to call you?'

He nodded and for a few seconds she saw clearly the vulnerable little unloved boy whose mother found him ugly.

'Oh Daniel, my darling,' she said.

Daniel bought the locket when he went into Canterbury. It was gold and heart-shaped with a scroll of delicate leaves on one side but plain on the other. It had been a good harvest and for some while now he had wanted to buy Betsy something really special. These days he often thought how blessed he was to have such a wife. He knew she was often sad about the baby she had lost. If he was honest with himself he accepted that it hadn't affected him in anything like the same way.

When she was first pregnant he had been glad that they were going to have a family, and for a while after her miscarriage he felt a spasm of disappointment when he thought about it. But he was much more concerned that Betsy herself was all right. Her unhappiness in the immediate aftermath was something he could only dimly imagine and it seemed that however hard he tried to console her she turned further from him.

He had been a little bothered too when Tom Shooter seemed to be always hanging around the kitchen, lingering after his meals ... after all the lad was a shining Greek god compared to himself. He had noticed how Tom watched her at the harvest supper. And *I was jealous,* he thought now, *jealous of his youth, his fair beauty, his tall, fine physique.* He saw them talking together at one stage, Betsy's face was flushed, her eyes sparkling blue fire and the pang of envy that shot through his body was something he had never before experienced. *What if she went off with the lad.* After all, she'd had no choice when taking him, but if the opportunity presented itself, would she go with the younger man?

Surely not, she loved him, Daniel Forrester, she had often told him so. Yet, seeing them standing together, he knew a devastation of emptiness that made him feel sick. *Oh Betsy, if I could I would lock you up where you saw no one who could tempt you.*

He knew that was impossible. She was his, not through choice, but because he had bought her, and the wonder of it all was that she gave herself and her love to him generously. In any case he loved her independence. He had never known a woman like her before. His mother was strong, but manipulating. The women he had bedded, and

70

there had been a few when he was a young lad, were pitiful compared to Betsy.

Her strength of will, her intelligence, her sense of the rightness of things, all these he loved, but more than anything she set his pulses and heart racing when she looked at him with love in her own eyes. Love for him. His thoughts returned to the harvest supper and that glimpse of his wife's animated face as she stood with Tom Shooter. People had moved in front of him while he was watching and when they moved away and he looked to where he had seen them talking both Betsy and Tom had disappeared from his view.

Daniel gave her the gold locket a few evenings afterwards and as he fastened it around her neck she whispered softly, 'It is too beautiful for me, Daniel, it must have cost so much.'

'Nothing is too beautiful for you, my darling, you have brought such happiness and love to my life. I would give you anything you wanted if I could, I love you so much.'

Tears filled her eyes as she thought that the one thing she desired now was a child of their own. He could give it to her but she seemed incapable of birthing it. But Betsy said nothing of this to her husband; she simply touched the locket and hugged him tightly to her breasts.

Two weeks later word came that Betsy's

mother had died. They set off for the funeral on a mellow September morning. Betsy did not pretend a sadness she didn't feel, only an annoyance that she would not now be able to find out if there was any reason for her miscarriages that her mother might have known about.

Afterwards Daniel took her back to the house for the funeral meal with the rest of the family. He felt very strongly that they should go. 'We do not need to stay long but it is right and proper that you should be there, Betsy,' he said, 'but as soon as you say the word after the meal is over we will leave.'

It felt strange being back in the old kitchen where she had toiled away while her brother and sisters seldom did any work. Certainly not any dirty work. She looked at the floor she had scrubbed so many times, remembered the scrubbed kitchen table and the uncomfortable stool where she had sat to peel potatoes and slice and wash vegetables.

She thought of her life after she left to work for Mrs Wallasey and of her life now in her own pleasant kitchen and around the farm with Daniel.

Her body was alive with the injustices she had suffered as a child, she even ducked out of the way when her brother walked in; she half-expected him to take a swing at her as he always used to. At first she had tried to fight back but it was an unequal contest and he made so much noise it always brought her mother along to side with him and clip her daughter's other ear, so in the end she gave up and simply endured it. Well, her mother would never again side with her brother, and she had Daniel to stand with her against them all. The only emotion she hadn't felt since returning here this morning was sorrow for the mother she had never loved and whom she was sure had never loved her. Her mother had not said so, like Daniel's mother who had undermined his confidence so cruelly, but it had been obvious by her attitude. Betsy had been just a servant in this house, a servant to them all. She had fought against the injustice of it but Daniel, in his childhood, had accepted and bowed down beneath it.

She seemed to hear her beloved Mrs Wallasey's voice saying, even as she had in life, 'We are all different, that's what makes humans so interesting Betsy – no two people ever tackle things in the same way.' Certainly she and Daniel had reacted quite differently to their environments and treatment.

Standing next to her mother's sister Agnes, Betsy thought, *well Aunt Agnes hasn't changed – she looks as sour as ever.* Agnes was her mother's only sister, the other three of that generation being boys. Even as a child Betsy had felt miserable whenever Agnes was present. The boys, her uncles, were mostly cheery men, but Agnes seemed to bring an aura of darkness with her. Once Betsy had left home she seldom thought about her aunt, but now, seeing her again the old feeling returned.

'So, you have a husband, eh? With your looks I would have thought you could have done better than *him*. What did he do – buy you in the market-place so he could parade a young and beautiful wife? Are your children like you or him?'

Determined not to be drawn into losing her temper on this occasion Betsy turned slightly as though she hadn't heard, but Agnes touched her arm and pulled her round so that they were face to face. 'You're like *him,* of course; not a touch of the Saldens in you.'

Agnes lowered her gaze first, as Betsy stared unbelievingly at her aunt. 'What exactly do you mean by that?' she said, fixing Agnes with the midnight blue of her eyes.

Ignoring her question her aunt said, 'He looked at me with your eyes once, until that night, crazy with drink, he bedded *her.*'

'Who? What are you talking about?' She gripped her aunt's arm until she made the woman wince.

'Get off. You've inherited his temper too. I don't know why you've come back here today, you never had time for any of us before–'

'What did you mean about his eyes and the Saldens? What are you hinting at?'

In her frustration she pinched her aunt's arm even harder and the woman pushed her roughly away. 'He was mine until she let him have his way with her. Just that once and I've *hated* you ever since.'

Wrenching herself free Aunt Agnes turned her back and went out of the room. Betsy stood perfectly still, a thousand thoughts chasing themselves around her mind. *Not a touch of the Saldens in you ... the night he bedded her...*

Who? Her mother. The venom in Agnes's voice made her shiver. Did that mean she had a different father from the others? Is that why she was always treated so badly?

She hurried after her aunt, determined to find the truth. She caught up with her in the kitchen. Everyone else was in the other room, chatting and reminiscing with each other as they ate and drank 'You must tell me – you've said too much not to finish now. Who was my father, why did my mother hate me so?'

With her back to the door in an effort to prevent her aunt's escape, her breath suddenly coming in short sharp bursts and her lovely eyes glittering with passion, she faced Agnes.

'Keep away. Keep away from me or I'll scream and they'll all come running. They know what he was like and you've inherited it. You're not one of us, you never have been.'

Betsy took a step closer. 'Go on.' It didn't sound like her own voice and Agnes looked round, but they were completely alone.

'All right. I vowed never to say but you've asked for it. Your father was *my* lover before he was hers. He took her one night in a drunken stupor. She did everything she could to lose you but nothing worked. When you were born she made us all promise not to tell the truth of the affair. You were her last fling – you were forced on her and she never forgave you or him. Now let me out of here.'

'One more question, then I will,' Betsy said with authority in her voice. 'Who was he? What was his name?'

'I can't – I won't tell you.'

'You *will* tell me. I have a right to know.' She took a step towards her aunt.

'All right, all right. His name was Choicely. He was the son of Sir Benjamin Choicely of Eccleton.'

Betsy realized that she was holding her breath and she let it go now in a rush of release. Moving from the door she waited until Agnes had scuttled through, then she sank on to the nearest chair.

Daniel found her there a few minutes later. 'I wondered where you were,' he said, 'suddenly I couldn't see you anywhere in the room. Are you all right?'

She grabbed his hand, 'Yes, I'm fine, Daniel, but let's go home now. I'm tired.'

He looked at her closely, but she turned her gaze away from him and stood up. Hand in hand they left the kitchen. She refused to return to the parlour where her brothers and sisters, aunt and uncles and cousins were. The din they were making was so great that none heard or saw Betsy and Daniel as the horse and cart rattled across the cobbles.

'Do you want to tell me what's happened?' Daniel said once they were moving gently through the countryside.

'When we're home. I can't talk about it now,' she managed before lapsing into silence. He whipped the horse into a trot, anxious to get her back.

She told him that evening. He held her close and said it didn't matter, she was Betsy, her own woman, that she had everything he had ever wanted. She looked at this man who had bought her in the marketplace, and knew now that if things had been different he was exactly whom she would have chosen to spend the rest of her life with.

In the early hours of the morning Betsy felt a great need to go to the lavatory. As she stumbled from the bed the movement woke Daniel and when she hadn't returned after ten minutes he went after her.

She was crumpled in a heap on the floor of the closet in the yard and quickly he knelt beside her. 'Betsy.' Gathering her in his arms he realized she was breathing. He carried her back to the bedroom and gently laid her on the covers. 'My darling, speak to me,' he whispered, rubbing her hands gently in his, 'what happened, what is it? Betsy, Bet...'

Her eyes opened – she seemed to have difficulty focusing on him but eventually she did and then her beautiful dark-blue eyes widened even more before filling with tears. 'Our baby. I've lost our baby,' she wailed.

The following night Betsy was delirious. Daniel sponged her hot face and body and tried to get her to have sips of water, but by morning he thought she was going to die. The raging temperature had gone but she lay limp and pale, and the only time she roused herself at all was when great bursts of sobbing racked her. After two days like this Daniel went for the doctor. He was worn out himself, with looking after her and the farm and getting very little sleep. As he harnessed the trap he said to the faithful farm-hand, 'I have to go out Jim, the missus is poorly. I'll fetch the doctor.'

Jim nodded. 'I'll stay around 'til you're back,' he said.

The doctor, a brisk no-nonsense man said

it happened all the time in childbirth and she simply needed to rest a bit, work a bit and stop feeling sorry for herself. 'And have another go quickly,' he added.

Very slowly Betsy recovered. Daniel tried to get her to talk about the baby. 'It was my fault for persuading you to go to the funeral,' he said one evening when they were sitting together. 'You hadn't wanted to go and none of this would have happened if–'

For the first time for weeks Betsy roused herself to something like her old passion. 'No Daniel, you were right that I should go. It's no use dodging unpleasant things. I'm glad now that I know the secret of my birth. I had no idea and it was a terrible shock but I've come to a decision.'

'And what's that, my darling.'

'I shall find my father – maybe not to tell him who I am but I want to see the stock I came from.'

'One question, Betsy. Why?'

Her beautiful eyes searched his face, then she said quietly, 'I never belonged in my family and I never knew why. This reason never entered my head, but now I do know I want to see the man who messed around with two sisters and fathered me. How many more of us are there? Has he a wife and family – a family who are half-related to me? I don't want to know them but I do want to know about them.'

Daniel sighed. He recognized the determination in his wife's voice and thought her search would probably bring her more anguish, yet he was so glad to hear her sounding more like his Betsy, fighting back instead of blaming herself for the loss of the baby he had not known she was expecting.

'I was going to tell you in another week or so,' she said the day after the miscarriage, 'it was at such an early stage and – and I wanted to be sure...' Her pale tear-streaked face haunted him still and if searching for the father she had just found out about would give her back her spirit he would go along with that.

Once Betsy had made her mind up to search for her father all her energies were directed towards the project. She returned to helping Daniel on the farm and all the while she was planning her next move in her quest. At first Daniel was co-operative but after a while he grew impatient with her. 'Why don't you leave it alone, Betsy?' he said one night. 'It's taking you over.'

'Can't you see I need to know?' she said. 'Maybe that's where this restlessness comes from, this need to get on. Perhaps it's inbred in my bones. Sir Benjamin Choicely. He's not from round here, is he, Daniel?'

'I've never heard of the man. I expect your aunt made the story up.'

'No,' she cried loudly, 'it was true. You can tell when someone is telling the truth. Well I can and Aunt Agnes was speaking the truth that day. Sir Benjamin Choicely's son, she said.'

'All right. I accept that. I can't see what finding him is going to prove or disprove.'

'I need to. I just need to. I never felt part of the family but I didn't know why. I don't *look* like any of them. And yet I never wondered, never thought. Now I want to explore the life of the man who fathered me. Is that wrong?'

'Not wrong Betsy,' Daniel said gently, 'but maybe not wise.'

She wrapped her arms around him, 'But I need to do this Daniel. I need to know, I really do.'

'Why?' But she had no answer for him.

She returned from the fields one day the following week and went into the farmhouse kitchen to find Daniel's brother Joseph there.

'Ah, the beauty herself,' he said, walking towards her. 'The beauty who married the beast.'

'Don't say things like that, Joseph.' She stood still as he reached her.

'But you wouldn't have married him of your own free will – you had no choice, did you? My brother bought you in the market-place, so let's have none of your high and mighty ways. You're a beauty though and if you're nice to me I'll see you all right. Pretty dresses to come out in and–' He got no further, for Betsy's hand was up and the stinging slap left his face smarting. *I seem to be doing a lot of this lately, she thought, what is it about me that makes men think I would be willing?*

'I am not a doll to be dressed in pretty clothes in return for my favours,' she said, 'and I am married to your brother. Now get out.'

'You're a fiery one – I like 'em with a bit of spirit. Come here, wench.' He reached forward. Betsy was too fast for him. She was off at speed and didn't stop until she was in the field next to where Daniel was working. *No, he has enough to do, she thought, I'll handle this one myself.* She turned and walked slowly back towards the farm.

Joseph was sitting on the ground by the corner which went round to the stable. He was leaning against the wall and watched her coming towards him.

'If you want your brother he's in the second field,' she called. 'Just keep away from the kitchen.' She went indoors and pushed the bolts of the door along.

A short while later she saw from the kitchen window Daniel stamping across the yard to where his brother was still sitting. She moved from the window so as not to be seen, then she unbolted the kitchen door. She thought her husband would kill his brother if he suspected anything and with the door locked and his knowledge of his brother's inclinations and reputation he would know.

She had no desire to protect Joseph but she knew Daniel's passionate temper and she wanted no man's blood on her conscience. The thought that Daniel might believe she had encouraged Joseph also crossed her mind. For all his strength he was vulnerable where relationships were concerned.

'I just hope Joseph isn't here for long,' she said to Dumbo. The cat had followed her indoors and was now rubbing round her skirt. 'He'll be wanting something, that's for sure, and I would have simply been a bonus.'

When Daniel and Jim came in for their meal Daniel said nothing about his brother and there was no sign of Joseph. Daniel didn't linger and went out with his cowman as soon as they had eaten. Often Jim went first, and she and Daniel were able to sit a few moments longer, sometimes in companionable silence and sometimes speaking and planning the afternoon's work.

Jim was never there for the evening meal and when they sat down for it that night, Daniel said his usual grace, 'For what we are about to receive may the Lord make us truly grateful.' Then, before he picked up his knife and fork, he said, 'How long had Joseph been hanging about this afternoon, Betsy?'

She had her answer planned. 'I don't really know, Daniel. I looked out of the kitchen window and saw you talking to him.'

'Did he come into the kitchen?'

'Why, no,' she answered truthfully.

'He said he had been in to see you and you told him where I was, so he waited.'

She was silent and looking across to her he said quietly, 'I was in the second field this afternoon and I sensed you were near, Betsy. I looked up and you were by the first field and hurrying away back here. Why was that?'

'Yes, I did see him,' she admitted. 'I was coming to tell you he was here, but then I realized how busy you were and came back before I reached the second field. I told him you were busy and I had cooking to do and went indoors. The next time I looked you were outside talking to him.'

'He – well, he hinted at certain things. Said he had been in to see my beautiful and seductive wife, and...' he laid down his cutlery and walked round to her side of the table, 'I didn't believe him but I was worried in case he had pestered you.'

His arm was round her shoulders now and she reached up and patted it tenderly, 'There's no need to worry, Daniel my love.

84

I learnt to deal with the likes of your brother years ago in service,' she said. Then she added for reassurance, 'He never came inside the kitchen.'

'He wanted money again,' said Daniel, and was it her imagination? Was there relief in his voice?

'You didn't–'

'Of course not. Joseph's money goes on women and drink. What we have is ours and he will never have a penny of it.' She felt his lips brush the side of her cheek, then he returned to his meal and began talking about the crops and the animals. A great feeling of love and protection for this man almost overwhelmed her. In spite of being so much younger than her husband she often felt years older and infinitely wiser in the ways of people.

'Daniel,' she said now, 'next market-day I will come with you and maybe I can find out something about Sir Benjamin Choicely and his son. I've been thinking about it a lot and I expect he came from these parts, don't you?'

Daniel drew his lips together in a hard line, then he looked across the table at her. 'You are determined to go through with this stupid idea, then?'

She nodded and knew immediately it was the wrong gesture, remembering too late how angry it had made him on that first day.

'Yes,' she said, quickly following up her action with speech. 'I simply want to know a little bit about him, that's all. Please try to understand, Daniel.'

He capitulated so suddenly it took her by surprise. 'I suppose I do in a way, but we are so different in our attitudes, Betsy. I would want to leave everything as it is, not try to disturb things, but you want to turf and dig until you know the truth about everything and sometimes this isn't good for anyone.'

She sent him a dazzling smile, and he felt again that surge of wonder that she was his. He knew he could not deny her anything she wanted for long.

That night she turned into his arms with an abandonment she hadn't shown him since that last miscarriage and her resultant illness.

Since her mother's funeral she had not communicated with the rest of her family, nor they with her. She knew that part of her life was over for ever, and in truth she had not enjoyed returning but Daniel's strong sense of duty and her desire to please him had been the driving force.

She sometimes felt guilty over her lack of feeling for her family when he talked about them but since the day of her mother's funeral she knew there was no need. Yet she could not help speculating about what

Benjamin Choicely and his son were like. Especially his son. From what her dreadful aunt had said she must resemble that side of her family. She couldn't say any of this to Daniel, but she began making plans for the big adventure of finding out about her father's family.

She talked to Dumbo about it sometimes when she had returned from helping her husband in the fields and the cat silently followed her into the house. He was never far from her and Daniel had taken to calling him her shadow. For her part she loved the creature dearly and when she was alone often rested her chin in his soft black fur and found comfort for the babies she had lost. Now she told the cat about her plans to find her father. 'I never knew the man I thought was my father, and I want to know something about the real one,' she murmured and felt Dumbo's body tremble in response.

When Daniel next went to market he said gruffly, 'Do you want to come, Betsy?'

'Yes. We need a few bits and I can get them while you are doing the business.'

They agreed to meet at noon. On the drive back Daniel said, 'A Sir Richard Choicely lives near Canterbury.'

'Richard, not Benjamin?'

'Benjamin was his father.'

She could have hugged him but she didn't

want him to drive off the road, so containing her excitement as best she could said, 'Oh Daniel, that's great news. Is he – is he married?'

'He was. He is a widower with two sons. But before you let your imagination go any further remember he may *not* be your father. Your mother could have been telling you the truth when she said your father died when you were a baby.'

'No, she wasn't. This makes sense. It explains why I was treated so differently from the rest of the family. Do you think they knew, Daniel, or – or...'

He slowed the horse a little and glanced at her set face. 'No, I'm sure they didn't. They took their lead from your mother in the way they behaved towards you. But there is no proof, Betsy. No proof at all. I only found out who he was and where he lived because you are so eager to know. I doubt if *he* will be and, true or not, he will probably deny the story anyway.'

That night she was awake long after their love-making finished and Daniel lay contentedly by her side. She was the daughter of Sir Richard Choicely – she should have been born to a grander life, a richer life. Her practical nature soon took over, however, and she reminded herself of Daniel's warnings. Of course he wouldn't acknowledge her, and yes, there was a part of her that accepted that the story might not be true. In her heart she was as sure as she could be that it was. Aunt Agnes couldn't play-act if she tried and on the day of the funeral she had blurted out the truth under her niece's questioning. Betsy was convinced about it.

She decided to mull the ideas around in her head for a few days. She had the information she needed now, and sometime in the future she would find out more. For the moment she was happy to have knowledge of Sir Richard's whereabouts. She fell asleep eventually, to dream of a large house with acres of grounds, and a happy family who never needed to wonder where the next meal was coming from as she often had before she went into service when she was ten years old.

Chapter 4

Three months after her discovery of where Sir Richard Choicely lived Betsy found a chance to satisfy some of her curiosity about him. She wanted to see if there was any truth in her aunt's words about the likeness but she knew Daniel was against any more delving.

'What good will it do you?' he said, 'Even

if it is so, and I don't believe it is, he is certain to deny it. You will make a laughing-stock of yourself, and Betsy, I couldn't bear that. You, who are so proud, and rightly so, surely you don't want to go begging a man to acknowledge you as his daughter if he has never done so before.'

She knew he was right and under normal circumstances she would feel the same but this was different. This involved her birth-right. This could answer her queries as to why she had always felt and been so differ-ent from her brothers and sisters.

'I shall not beg him to acknowledge me, Daniel, I shall only ask to be told the truth. I am not asking him for anything except one fact.'

It was when a horse bolted in the lane that the miracle happened. It seemed like a miracle to Betsy. The rider was injured and Daniel helped him into the house, the horseman leaning heavily on the smaller man. Together Daniel and Betsy tended his wounded leg, then Daniel went to get the trap to take him home. The horse had been caught by their neighbour, Martin, and while he and Daniel were harnessing the trap and capturing the runaway horse the injured man was sitting in Betsy's kitchen telling her how grateful he was to them.

'Where do you live? Is it far?' she asked

'A few miles this side of Canterbury, at Sir

Richard Choicely's place.'

She could not believe it at first, but before she had formed one of the many questions she wanted to ask him the men were back and helping the rider outside. There was no further opportunity, for it was obviously a painful process for the injured man and she could see him sweating with the effort. Quickly she made her decision and hurried to fetch her cloak and bonnet. She pulled on her boots, bolted the back door and ran into the yard, where the men had at last got the injured rider into the trap and reasonably comfortable. Martin was going to ride the man's horse. Whatever had startled the animal into bolting seemed to have had no ill-effects, for he was calm and easily handled now.

'Betsy, what are you doing?'

'I shall come with you, Daniel. I can help because it might be a bumpy ride for someone with an injured leg. I have brought a rug and bolted the door.'

She could tell Daniel was not pleased, but, obviously anxious to get the injured man home quickly, he said nothing, simply clambered into the driving-seat and set off. It was a long drive and would have been such an opportunity for her to find out a little of Sir Richard Choicely's way of life, but the injured man had his eyes closed most of the time and Betsy was aware of her husband's disapproval of her having come with them. Their patient did tell them he was on his way back home, having been to visit a sick relative for two days, so the horse was well rested for the journey.

Betsy kept silent when Daniel, following his passenger's directions, eventually turned into the drive of Chasebury, Richard Choicely's estate. As Daniel and Martin helped the injured rider down and half-carried him into the house Betsy sat quietly in the trap. She was longing to go inside too, but knew it would be foolish to antagonize her husband by doing so. On the occasions when they clashed she felt miserable and upset. This surprised her but it was a fact and in her straightforward fashion she acknowledged this.

Her thoughts at this moment were exciting. Only a few hours ago she had not known where Sir Richard lived, and now, although etiquette and her husband's temper meant she was denied the chance she craved, here she was outside his grand-looking home. Truly fate was often strange, and sometimes kind as well. Her body trembled with emotions which she fought to control, bringing a flush to her cheeks and even more sparkle to her eyes, the eyes that Aunt Agnes said were 'his eyes'.

Daniel and Martin were not long in the house and when they emerged it was with another man, who walked over to the trap with them.

'This is my wife, Mistress Betsy Forrester,' Daniel said, and Richard Choicely, for it was indeed he, took her hand.

'You have all been very kind,' he said, 'my steward is being attended to now and he too is grateful for your help.' He moved back as Daniel and Martin climbed aboard, and then they were off. Betsy bit her lip and seethed with frustration because, although she had now seen Richard Choicely she had not had a chance to – to what, she wondered. She could hardly say to him, 'Are you my father?'

Nevertheless the ice was broken and she had actually met the man. If she could devise a way to be somewhere where he was going to be during the next few weeks or months, then anything was possible. On the journey home she tried to keep the impression of his face in her mind but it proved singularly difficult. The only clear thought she had was that she did not resemble him in any recognizable manner.

After they had left Martin at his farm they went on in silence. Once the horse was stabled and the trap housed for the night Daniel came into the parlour where she was making a fuss of Dumbo. She jumped up to greet her husband, excitement shining through her eyes.

'Are you satisfied now you've seen him,' he said shortly.

'Yes, Daniel. It would have been nice to talk to him for a while, or even go inside and meet the rest of the family.'

She said it mischievously knowing he would retaliate, but she wasn't prepared for the next revelation.

'I refused.'

At first she thought she had not heard him correctly, but one look at his face told her that her husband was telling the truth.

'You refused? You mean you had the chance, *I* had the chance, to go inside and talk and you ... you...'

Words failed her and she clenched her fists at him. 'What right do you have to refuse, to turn down what might have been the chance of a lifetime for me?'

He glanced towards the straw halter but she was so worked up that the significance of the movement passed her by.

'Just listen to yourself,' he said, 'listen to how you're carrying on. That alone proves I was right not to let you get inside the house and ask him questions. Wild questions which might not have a grain of truth about them.'

'They have, they have,' she cried passionately. 'Oh why did you turn down such an opportunity? It meant nothing to you but it means so much to me. You're a selfish, mean man Daniel ... and I hate you.'

He came towards her then, and he was laughing as he pulled her close to him. 'You are magnificent when you are as angry as this,' he said, his voice hoarse with passion, and tugging impatiently at her skirts he almost flung her on to the settee in his excitement.

Angrily she pushed him away, but he overpowered her and began covering her face and neck with kisses. She resisted for only a few seconds more before she capitulated, wanting him as much as he needed her.

Richard Choicely went thoughtfully indoors after the trap had gone. That woman, the farmer's wife, was so beautiful. There was a fire sparking in her eyes and a warm glow radiating from her cheeks and lips. She reminded him of someone, yet he knew he had never seen her before. Unless it was in a painting but he could not recall which one. There had been a vibrancy about the woman, that dark glossy hair, those eyes that seemed to be dancing with bright mischief, and that superb figure.

Her dress beneath the open cloak had been simple and homespun. She wore it with the air of a lady, and the tantalizing glimpse of a creamy cleavage as her shawl trembled slightly when she moved to greet him sent a sliver of excitement throughout his being.

He shook his head in disbelief. Whatever was he thinking of, she was a farmer's wife who had come along on this errand of mercy to enliven her dull existence. Yet in his mind's eye he could picture her at a grand ball, in a dress of finest silk or taffeta, her lithe body moving in rhythm with his.

'Stop,' he said aloud, 'you're mad. Such thoughts.' Deliberately he pictured Lily, the young lady to whom he was betrothed. Her skin was as pale and smooth as the finest porcelain, her voice and manner charming, yet – yet she did not intoxicate him as that glorious beauty whom he had just encountered had done with one rather demure glance. He was sure his heart had doubled its normal beat when their hands had briefly touched.

Since his wife's death, three years before, Richard had not been celibate, but now the time had come to take himself a new wife. He needed someone to be hostess at the dinners, someone by his side officially.

Lily was twenty years younger than he was and she came from good stock. The Aston-Jenkins were landowners of substance and well thought of. Although not a great beauty, Lily had style and panache. He did not love her as he had loved his wife but she and her family had accepted him and he did not doubt that they would have a happy life together.

Much later that night, in his lonely bed, he awoke from a dream about the farmer's wife, the beautiful Betsy Forrester he had met for the first time earlier in the day. As he turned towards her she melted into the softness of the sheets and the space beside him was empty. He groaned aloud.

The daily round back at the farm occupied a lot of Betsy's time, yet still she thought about that glimpse of the man whom she believed to be her father. It was all very well for Daniel to say it probably wasn't so, but there was at least as much chance that it was, although she had to admit she had not detected a likeness.

'I wasn't looking for one,' she told Dumbo as she busied herself in the bedroom one day. The old cat, as usual had followed her upstairs and was sitting on the wicker basket in the corner of the room. 'Maybe it is an inherited thing, the way I lose the baby each time I'm pregnant. I need to know if there is a connection yet Daniel simply won't see it that way.'

She pulled the cover back over the bed and sighed. Her life had changed so much since her marriage and it was all to the good. Daniel respected her mind and they had such wonderful discussions about almost everything under the sun, she sometimes thought. He allowed her an opinion. If he didn't agree with it he said so and he never shouted at her when she took a different point of view from his own. The only bone of contention was made of straw.

The halter hung steadfastly on the hook and recently Betsy had tried to imagine it as a straw necklace. Maybe this bitter bile that rose in her throat if she allowed her thoughts to linger on it would stop if she could change the picture of it in her mind.

It wasn't easy but she refused to dwell on the prospect that her husband left it there in case he should want to return her and let someone else one day lead her from the market-place. She knew Daniel harboured no such thoughts, she loved and trusted him, they were partners in their husband-and-wife relationship, not master and servant as in so many marriages. Yet the halter was the one thing he would not discuss. Nor would he move it.

'It stays,' he thundered at her one day. 'I need it.' He looked so menacing and as he turned quickly away and strode across the room he did look and sound ugly, his normally gentle voice hoarse with a passionate anger. She could not understand why it meant so much to him. He, who gave generously over everything else would not give her this one thing that he knew she longed for.

That row had lasted longer than most of their little skirmishes. For three nights she turned her back and moved far over to the edge of the bed, and when he rolled towards her she roughly pushed him back. Yet he didn't even try to take her, simply returned to his side of the double bed.

The days were almost normal because Daniel was out in the fields and Jim the farm-hand was there at midday. They were cool with each other but they spoke and the situation did not develop into a silence or more arguments. Yet she knew the matter was settled. Over the straw halter he had proved to be the master.

The night when Sadie the cow died was when they once again curled into each other's arms. She had been poorly for several days and Jim reported that she was ''bout the same,' shaking his young head and looking sadder than usual before he left, well after his normal time.

Daniel returned to look at her after his meal on Saturday evening. He was gone longer than Betsy expected and she went to see what was happening. They had isolated Sadie, putting her into a shed with lots of straw and water and Daniel was there on his hands and knees beside the creature and talking to her.

He looked up as Betsy came over. 'Nothing more we can do for her,' he said quietly.

Squatting beside him she touched the cow's flanks.

'Poor old thing,' she said, 'Will any of the others be infected?'

'No. She has milk-fever. Jim and I have tried everything. Meg is suckling her calf and she's doing fine.'

Betsy stayed for an hour, then returned to the house and poured two drinks which she took back with her.

'Thanks.' He drank some then turned to her, 'I love you, Betsy,' he said.

'And I love you too, Daniel.' She leaned forward and there beside the dying cow, their lips met in a brief kiss. An hour later Sadie suddenly gave a huge sigh and breathed her last. Daniel and Jim buried Sadie very early on Sunday morning and Betsy went into the field and watched the tiny calf lying down with Meg.

Next market-day Betsy went with Daniel, and although she watched for Sir Richard Choicely or his retainer, she did not see them.

Richard Choicely was sitting in the window-seat of the Roebuck Inn when Betsy and Daniel stopped outside. They were talking and laughing together and again, as he had done that night when they had brought his steward back after the accident, he thought what a beauty the woman was.

He recognized her immediately, and as neither of them was looking his way he allowed his gaze to wander from her glorious dark hair to her finely turned ankles, which were just showing beneath her dress. Her face and figure were superb, he thought. She reminded him of someone. Probably an actress whom he had seen.

'Hello, Richard. I'm a bit late, the business took longer than I thought. Have you ordered?' Reluctantly Richard Choicely turned from the window to greet his friend William. When he looked back a few seconds later Betsy and Daniel were touching hands then each went off in different directions.

Following his gaze William said, 'She is a beauty, isn't she. Got your eye on her?'

'Of course not. It is just that she reminds me of someone but I cannot think whom.'

'She looks like a younger version of your mother to me. Noticed her as I came in. Ravishing. An absolute stunner.'

Business and eating took up the next hour or so for Richard, and it wasn't until he was on the homeward run that he thought again about the girl in the market-place. Of course William was right, she *did* look a bit like his mother. More than a bit, uncannily like her.

When he reached home and divested himself of his garments he poured himself a whiskey and went into the long gallery to look at the painting of his mother which was hanging there along with the other Choicely family portraits.

The likeness was unmistakable. His thoughts flew back twenty years to his brother Benjamin. Was it possible? There had been talk about a rough woman from one of the villages arriving one day and demanding to see him. She made such a fuss that his father eventually spoke to her. What he told her Richard never knew, except that the woman went away and they never saw her again, but he heard the rumours circulating among the servants that: 'Young Benjamin's been at it again and this one means business.'

Only a month later Ben had been killed in a horse-riding accident. It was an unusual accident to befall an experienced rider because no one else seemed to be involved and there were no trees or obstacles lying in his path to have caused his horse to stumble.

Sir Benjamin and Lady Choicely were devastated and for a while Lady Helen went into a decline. Ben was her firstborn and favourite child. Richard had known this since he was a small boy and understood it to be because he was the heir to the Choicely estate. As he grew older he discovered another reason for her preference. The young Benjamin was the image of his mother's father, whom she had adored, whereas he, Richard, had inherited his father's looks and temperament.

The two brothers were as unlike each other as could be. Benjamin's hair had a gleaming blackness like his mother's, his eyes were almost navy-blue and dancing with merriment, even when he was a child. Richard's sandy-coloured hair imitated his father's and his grey-green eyes were, he knew, more serious than Ben's twinkling ones that seemed to get him anything he wanted. When Benjamin Choicely died in that freak accident Richard became the heir apparent.

Now he wondered about the girl. She appeared to be the right age and the more he pictured her in his mind's eye the more he saw the family likeness. He had never known his maternal grandfather but his mother would relate tales of heroic deeds credited to him and as a young child he often wished he had the black hair and laughing eyes that came down through that side of the family. It seemed to open the door to so much that was fun, and the young Richard would have liked more of that. As it was he was cast as the intellectual boy and in truth even that had been hard work.

He struggled with studies to please his parents, to gain a little more of their attention and praise. It never worked for him. He was a good horseman but Ben was a brilliant one. He was a proficient archer but Ben was better. He was an admirable cricketer but Ben was an inspired one. The only thing he outshone his brother in was gentleness and that was not a quality that counted for a great deal in the Choicely family.

He was known in the servants' quarters as the caring son; he knew this because the cook mentioned it one day when he had been particularly upset over a treat that he had been promised and which was stopped because he had answered his father back. Not that he had told her, but she seemed to know just the same.

''Tis a crying shame,' she said, as she set a glass of homemade lemonade before him in the kitchen. 'That young scoundrel Ben would have got away with it. But don't you fret, Master Richard, we all know your worth down here. You're the caring one and in the long run that's what will count. Your brother may be having the best of it now but he'll get his comeuppance one day, you'll see.'

He used to spend a great deal of time below stairs then, but was careful not to let his parents know because he knew it would be banned. Often when they thought he was out roaming the grounds he had sneaked back in through the laundry door of the servants' quarters where he always felt welcome. In later years, when he succeeded to the baronetcy he thought it had helped him enormously to fulfil his duties because he knew and understood the working people so well.

If, and it is a very big if, he told himself – but *if* that girl is Ben's daughter she may have a claim to the estate. Not a legitimate one because of the circumstances of her birth, but a claim in his eyes, nevertheless. The gentle one had inherited something from the maternal side of his family, even if it was not their dark good looks and vivacity. That was self-preservation. If the girl was who she undoubtedly *could* be, he wanted to find out quietly. After all, his brother had been the elder and he had left no heirs. Could this be an unofficial heiress? If the position had been reversed he knew Ben would have laughed and denied it, and as she was illegitimate she would have no legal rights, but if she *was* his brother's daughter and his niece Richard wanted to know.

Chapter 5

Richard Choicely made a few discreet enquiries about Betsy Forrester, the farmer's wife. His findings neither proved nor disproved his suspicions about her being his brother's child.

He discovered that a certain George Hatton had had a wife who was much younger than he, but no children. He learned that he also was a farmer, but here his information stopped. No one was able to tell him in what way Betsy Forrester had been connected to Hatton.

He did not visit the farmer, feeling that it would be inappropriate for a man of his standing. He did not let the mystery go however, and quietly pursued his quest through others whenever he had the opportunity.

It was some weeks after this that he discovered the girl who was haunting his thoughts had once worked in Wren Court which was but an hour's drive away from Chasebury Manor. Much closer than where the farmer Hatton lived. Richard decided to pay a visit to Wren Court.

John Wallasey, who still lived there with his wife Sarah, at first denied any knowledge of her. 'Servants come and go,' he said, but eventually he confirmed, with prompting from Sarah, that a child called Betsy had once worked for his late mother. They both said they had no idea where she had come from before that, nor what had happened to her. Richard had to accept this but felt sure they knew more than they told.

With his fondness for chatting to the servants however, he discovered that Betsy's name before her marriage had been Salden. He extended his detective work to several nearby villages, gradually widening his area until he learned of a family of that name who lived in Marshdean.

Other business interests prevented him from doing much for a while and it was almost six months and well into autumn when he donned a peasant's outfit for a trip to Marshdean. He did not travel in the carriage but in the pony and trap.

'Put me down just outside the village and give me a couple of hours,' he told John, his driver, 'then pick me up here.'

He strode away, walking at a brisk pace. It was noon, the weather was mild and pleasant and he felt excited about this expedition to uncover the mystery. In his youth he hadn't really mourned his brother for they were never close, but now he wanted to find out because he could not seem to get the farmer's wife out of his mind for long. And he found the family likeness to his mother uncanny.

When he came to the George and Dragon he went in. It was well patronized but not crowded. He ordered a beer and bread and cheese. Sitting at the bar he looked around before selecting a thin man with dull grey hair and a short to middling grey beard, who appeared to be alone. He took his drink and food across to the table.

'Mind if I join you,' he said.

'Suit yourself,' the man replied. He looked to be in his fifties or sixties and if he was a villager he was likely to know the family.

'I'm a stranger here but I'm looking for a family called Salden,' Richard said. 'I was told they came from these parts. Don't know them by any chance, do you?'

'Can't say as I do. Why d'you want to know.'

Richard was expecting this one. 'I have a message for one of them. She's called Betsy Salden.' He watched the old man's eyes and face as he said the name and had the satisfaction of seeing a glimmer of recognition.

'No, never 'eard of 'em.'

Richard indicated his three-quarters finished ale. 'Let me get you some more,' he said, rising from his seat.

Twenty minutes later he left the inn, armed with the knowledge he wanted. 'Big family,' his informant had told him. 'Couldn't tell you the names of most of 'em but Betsy, she stood out. Real beauty she was for all she was so young.'

'Young, how young?'

'Just a kid. Nine or ten. Went into service somewhere. Used to come home once a year and she made yer mouth water she did. Never saw her much after she turned fourteen or fifteen. Some of the family's still about, though I did hear the mother died last year. She could have been good-looking in her youth, I shouldn't wonder, but nine or ten kids did for her.' He chuckled suddenly.

'Nice drop of ale they serves here.' Richard walked to the bar and bought him another.

The man slurped noisily. 'Thank ye. What's your business with 'em?'

'Knew them years ago. I've been travelling and wondered how they were. Would you know where they're living now?'

'Still at the old place, far as I know.'

Richard, who had noticed many flower names for the cottages as he walked down the street, said, 'I could never remember the name of their cottage, but it's down the bottom there, isn't it? Violet or Ivy or something.'

'Rose,' the old man said, almost bursting with information now his thirst was being regularly sated. 'On the left in Wicket Lane at bottom of hill. Did hear there was a to-do about it after the old lady died. She was the tenant see, but one of the older children and his family took it over. Bit of fighting about it. Betsy Salden,' he mused softly, 'Mm-mm. Not seen 'er fer years. She didn't come back to the village I know that. You wouldn't miss a girl with her looks.'

Richard thanked him and left. He followed the main street where the pub was for a few hundred yards and, following the old man's instructions, turned into the lane on the left. Halfway down he found what he was looking for: Rose Cottage, which stood out from its neighbours by its dereliction.

There were no flowers in the small garden as in some of the others, and the yellowing grass was long.

Richard approached the front door. He had planned what to say and when after a few moments a voice from the yard where the back door was situated called irritably, 'What d'you want?' he made to go towards it.

'We don't want nothing.' The voice was surly and the door banged shut. Richard stood for a moment contemplating his next move when it suddenly opened again. An unkempt and unshaven man blocked the entrance, 'You don't look the begging sort. What you come for?'

He obviously hoped it was to give them something good, and regretted his first instinctive slamming of the door.

'I'm looking for Betsy Salden.'

The man spat. 'What for?'

'I knew her years ago. Wondered if she was still here.'

The man cackled noisily. 'Not her. Never come near the place once 'er mother kicked the bucket. Good riddance too, I say. Too 'igh an' mighty ever since she were little.' His eyes narrowed. 'What you want 'er for? You got some money for 'er, then?'

Richard smiled – he'd thought as much when the man called him back. Good job he didn't look anything like Ben or Betsy, who, he was becoming surer than ever now, was his brother's daughter by this Salden woman who died last year.

'No. Just wanted to look her up for old times' sake.' He moved swiftly down the path, aware that the man was watching intently. He tried to slouch and not appear to stride out, to make it seem he was simply a wanderer and not a man with a purpose.

Once more in the lane he kept up the gait so as not to arouse suspicion. The last thing he wanted was for them to associate the girl with the Choicelys. If she turned out to be Ben's child he wanted to know. He wasn't sure yet what he would do, but he would certainly see that she was never destitute. He turned back into the main street, where he met no one as he walked to the end of the village, although he didn't doubt for one moment that there were people who saw him and wondered who he was. It was a further mile to where the pony and trap would be waiting – he had told his driver to go off on his own and not stay close until it was time to collect him. The trap was there waiting and soon they were heading for Chasebury Manor.

During the next few days Richard found out a lot more about Betsy Salden. He now knew she had gone to work for Mrs Wallasey when she was ten and had been married to George Hatton at barely fifteen. Quite how she became Daniel Forrester's wife he wasn't sure, but the most likely explanation was that George had sold her. Richard could not understand why: a lovely woman like that, but it seemed the only logical thought. Unless she had run away from George Hatton and Daniel had rescued her. The more he thought about it the more likely that seemed to him. His natural curiosity coupled with his love of research took over and he determined to find out more about the life of the beautiful woman who could possibly be his niece.

His logical mind looked at every aspect of the situation. On physical appearance alone the idea was feasible – he had the portrait of his late mother taken down from the wall and studied it from every angle. Those dark-blue fathomless eyes, that midnight-black hair, the skin colouring, which Richard thought the artist had captured perfectly in the painting, it all matched. No wonder that girl had looked familiar when he first saw her. She was like a younger edition of the mother he remembered coming into the nursery when he was a child.

Although he did not have it taken down he went on several evenings after dinner to the long gallery and looked on his brother Benjamin's portrait. The likeness was there too, especially when you knew what you were looking for. Again his astute mind searched for snags but found none. He tried to picture the girl with her long hair cut to just below her ears, with a man's body stature instead of a woman's and grinned ruefully when he realized that man or woman, both Ben and Betsy seemed to have the charisma that made folk remember them for their beauty.

That was another thing, her name. Betsy. He wondered if her mother had deliberately given her a name beginning with the first two letters of his brother's, but he dismissed this as too fanciful. He wished he had a portrait of Betsy to compare with the others, but he only had the impressions in his mind.

He returned to the library, fetched some paper and pens and tried to draw the girl. He had been a reasonable artist in his youth although Ben's drawings and paintings were the ones that found their way to his mother's treasure-chest. Now he mentally tossed that rather bitter memory away, as his pencil rapidly sketched the high cheekbones, the small nose, the long hair and the glorious figure of the woman he had seen only twice in his life.

Richard Choicely sank into the deep armchair. On the small table by his side was a drink and on his lap a sketch-pad with various drawings of Betsy Forrester. He sipped and savoured the brandy, gazing all the while at what he had drawn. There was no doubt she had many of the features of his mother's side of the family, the Beaumonts. How he hadn't seen it was his mother of whom she reminded him, he didn't know. William had noticed it immediately, so it definitely wasn't imagination on his part.

Recalling the time when the village woman had come to Chasebury Manor Richard tried to remember what he knew, which had been precious little at the time. He realized Ben was in serious trouble but his elder brother seemed to thrive on it. This time, though, there had seemed to be real concern in the family. He recalled the talk in the servants' quarters. It always stopped when he appeared, but he heard enough to know something was afoot.

In retrospect, remembering snatches of conversations he wasn't meant to hear, and picturing the scenes between his parents, he was sure that this was Benjamin's child and the woman was her mother. What had she hoped for when she came to Chasebury? Money most probably, or recognition for her daughter. Was the beautiful Betsy that child? Those memories were hazier than the ones of his brother's death, which occurred not so long afterwards. As he stroked the brandy-glass he let the memories run through his mind again, like a well-remembered play.

Ben had gone riding early in the morning.

He did this most days and he was usually gone for several hours. Later that afternoon his horse was seen in the woods over a mile away and the search for him began. They found him in a clearing half a mile from the house, dead, with head wounds and a broken back.

His mother was inconsolable and took to her room, refusing to see anyone but her husband when he took her food to her. Sir Benjamin went around the place, carrying on his duties but with such a forbidding air that the young Richard kept out of his way.

Recalling that time now he found the snatches of talk among the servants were clear in his memory. *'Not a natural accident, Pike says there was some rope stretching between two trees.'* This had been cook and the butler speaking about Pike the gamekeeper.

'Foul play – mind, he had his enemies. There's many a wench round these parts whose lives he's ruined. I know one from the village as nearly died a few months ago when she was in trouble.'

Yes, there had been lots of such conversations which mysteriously stopped when he appeared in the kitchen. His young mind must have registered not only the words but the expressions and tones of voice, for he could picture the scenes as clearly as if it had all happened yesterday instead of all those years ago. He wondered now about that rope stretched between two trees. That servants' gossip he had picked up on must have embedded itself deeply in his mind and was being triggered now by a beautiful and familiar face seen in the market-place.

Had the woman who had left Chasebury without anything for her child taken a terrible revenge on the man who fathered it? If only Pike were still alive. Suddenly he remembered that Pike had had a son. If he wasn't mistaken that son was now gamekeeper to Charles Dicton at Pensfield. His hands lovingly circled the brandy-glass and he smiled to himself. He would pay Charles a visit just as soon as he could.

It was nearly ten days later before Richard found the time to take the twenty-six mile trip to Pensfield. He travelled with his coachman and they put up at an inn for the night. The following morning he sent a note to Sir Charles Dicton and less than an hour later the two men were greeting each other. At first the talk was about the land, the king, the government, but eventually Richard asked about the gamekeeper.

'Yes, Jim Pike's with me. A good man.'

'As was his father,' Richard said. 'He was with my father for many, many years. I should like to have a word with Jim about his dad if that is possible while I'm in the area. I remember him as a little lad, of course. We are about the same age.'

'His cottage is along the lane. Primrose

Cottage. Third one along from here.' The men parted on convivial terms and Richard made his way to the gamekeeper's home. He was in luck as Jim Pike was indoors. The two men spoke of many things to do with game and country matters before Richard broached the reason he had come.

'Jim, did your father ever speak to you about my brother Benjamin's accident?'

Jim shot him a wary look, then nodded his head slowly.

'I'm checking a few things from the past, Jim. Ben was a superb horseman and no other rider was involved, yet something threw him that day.' Jim continued to look at him without speaking, and Richard said, 'I was a child at the time, yet I heard rumours. I didn't fully understand their meaning then, of course, but thinking about it all now I am wondering whether it was an accident or something more sinister. Will you tell me what your father told you?'

'No harm to now, I s'pose.' Jim drew his lips together into a sucking movement, sending lines running up his weatherbeaten face. ''Twas when he were ill, not long afore he died when he mentioned it. "Jim," he says, "I'm going to tell you something I wouldn't have believed if I hadn't seen it with me own eyes, lad."'

'Go on,' Richard said into the silence which followed the gamekeeper's words.

117

'"A few yards from where young Ben lay there was a rope stretched between two trees. I rushed to Ben, of course, but he were dead and I went straight to the big house and when I went back to the wood afterwards the rope had gone."'

'Gone?'

'That's right, gone. That's what me dad said. No sign of it at all, so he didn't mention it to anyone.'

'What else did he tell you, Jim?'

'Said it played on his mind a bit – you know – that someone had deliberately tied it across.'

'Well, thanks, Jim. It's too long ago now to follow it up, of course, but it looks as though someone set out to kill my brother, doesn't it?'

'It's what me dad thought. He said the horse would be going too fast there to stop.' As Richard rose and extended his hand the gamekeeper said, 'There was one more thing he told me. When he went back, while the others were with your poor brother, who had been taken up to the house, he stood looking round for the rope which wasn't there any more.'

Richard held his breath as Jim Pike paused dramatically and rubbed his big hand against his chin. 'As he moved away he saw the back of a woman hurrying through the trees. He ran after her but she dodged him

118

and he never saw her face.'

'He had no idea, I suppose, who she might be?'

'No. He said she had a black shawl or something round her head and shoulders. He never told the master or mistress because they were in such a state. He did ask what time the accident was, though. You know, if he'd been lying there dead a long while, and Sir Benjamin told him the doctor said it had only just happened before they arrived, even though he'd been out all morning. It seemed he was on his way back...'

Richard thanked him and took his leave. He returned thoughtfully to his carriage and home. Had Betsy's mother killed the man responsible, and because Pike came along looking for him at that point she had had no time to take down the evidence until he went to fetch help? It looked suspiciously as though that were the case. Now she was dead he would never know the truth. The old man at the cottage in Marshdean would probably know, might even have helped tie the rope, but he'd never admit it.

The village of Marshdean wasn't far from Chasebury Manor, especially if you cut through the woods, and it would have been as easy for any of the girls from there to meet Ben as it was for those from several other hamlets in the area.

Richard shuddered, suddenly wondering if

he wanted to pursue this any more. What was it that that greedy man had said to him the day he went to the village, 'You got some money for 'er then?' He was one of the Saldens, her mother's brother maybe, which would make him Betsy's uncle, the same as me, he thought, if my workings out are anywhere near the truth.

Forcing his mind back through the years he recalled that Ben's horse, Strike, although uninjured, had been shot afterwards. Knowing about the rope now he thought the horse had probably pulled up sharply on seeing it, Ben had been thrown and the horse had galloped back the way it had come. He remembered how upset he had been when he knew that Strike had been killed, and the warmth of the comfort he found in the kitchens of Chasebury Manor, while his parents upstairs cried for their elder son.

Chapter 6

During the winter Betsy concentrated on her fight for women to be recognized as equals and partners to men. She wrote letters to the papers, to members of parliament and to anyone in public life who she thought could help her cause.

Daniel supported her in these efforts and although she still hoped they would have a child she tried to take a realistic view and accept that it might not happen. It wasn't easy. Loving him as she did she wanted to bear his children. What was wrong with her that she hadn't been able to? Her heart told her she hadn't conceived when she was with George Hatton because he forced himself on her, but her thinking told her that it would have made no difference. It was a natural happening. *I'm a simple country girl,* she told herself, *but I have been taught how to use my mind, and there is a reason somewhere. I'm not educated enough to find it.* Nevertheless she took comfort from the fact that three times now she had found herself with child.

She quietly mourned for those lost children but she kept these thoughts to herself, and would have been surprised if she could have seen into Daniel's mind sometimes when he observed her in these moments and felt her sadness but did not know what to do to ease it.

Why do I lose my babies, she wrote in her notebook, for she had returned to writing down some of her thoughts as she used to do for Mrs Wallasey. *Maybe the answer to that is to do with my father because my mother managed to have many children.*

She wrote a passionate piece about edu-

121

cating girls *because they are the mothers of all the country's children and if they are educated and respected they in turn will do the same for their sons and daughters and life will be fairer for everyone.*

She even wrote to the king decrying the practice of public wife-selling. Not knowing how to address him she simply put: *To King George, Will you do something to stop the barbaric practice of buying a wife in the market as if she was a sack of flour?* She did not receive a reply.

She did have answers to a few of her other letters, however. Some from like-minded people and some from folk who wanted no change in the treatment of men and women. *But then, the girls it happens to are usually the ones who cannot read and write,* she confided to the notebook. *I can and I must use my knowledge to help them.* She formed a bond and exchanged letters with the ones who answered but neither she nor any of them were in a position to do something about the situation just now.

'But the time will come,' she said to Daniel when they discussed the matter, 'and teaching all children to read and write is the beginning of it.'

Employing her energy in the fight for a better deal for women went some way to putting the episode with Tom Shooter behind her.

In between her letter-writing and managing the house and dairy she was often out with Daniel and Jim seeing to the animals during a bad winter.

At the beginning of December Joseph rode over to say the older Mrs Forrester was ill and he couldn't manage. Apart from the animals it was quiet at this time of year on the farm and Daniel went over to see his mother, but on the second day he returned.

'The farm is in a dreadful state,' he told Betsy. 'Everything falling to pieces around them. That lazy brother of mine has only ever been interested in having a good time and apparently our mother has been ailing for some weeks and has let things go. Will you come with me tomorrow? We can leave Jim here to see to things and the dairymaid can manage on her own for the day.' The dairymaid lived with her parents and younger siblings in one of the four cottages at the end of the lane.

They took some provisions with them and while Betsy cleaned and cooked Daniel helped Joseph with repair jobs around the farm and house. He was careful to be indoors when his brother was there, never leaving him alone with Betsy.

They came home that evening but returned the following day to Sandilands Farm. Mrs Forrester seemed a little better. 'That's because of your good food and attention,' Daniel said to Betsy.

It was as she was leaving the bedroom later that afternoon, having taken her mother-in-law some soup and waited while the old lady slowly drank it, that she encountered Joseph on the steep, narrow stairs. Instinctively she pulled herself into the side and he said quietly, 'Come on, Betsy, one little kiss won't hurt.'

'You touch me, Joseph and I'll push you to the bottom of the stairs. I mean that.'

She saw the uncertainty in his eyes and pressed home her advantage. 'Keep your hands off and let me pass. I don't give second chances,' she said. To her great relief he did just that and she went down the stairs and into the kitchen with the invalid's soup bowl.

It was another week before the old lady was up and once more in charge of the farm and her kitchen. Betsy and Daniel drove over in the trap for part of each day, Daniel always did some things on his own farm first because he said it wasn't fair to leave too much to Jim. Betsy left soup and bread and cheese and sometimes a piece of apple-pie for Jim's lunch. He stayed willingly enough and Betsy later confided to her notebook. *Jim is the best there is. How would we have managed without him?*

On the last day they were at Sandilands Daniel's mother grudgingly thanked them for helping out. 'Now I'm on me feet, Joseph will work,' she said. 'I'll make him.'

Betsy did not doubt that when she came in from feeding the hens and overheard her shouting at her younger son. 'Getting that bastard brother of yours over here, you lazy sod. From now on you do your share here, I've had enough of giving in to you. You'll get nothing more from me if you don't pull yer weight. I could've died while you sat on yer bum and let me.'

Daniel injured his ankle on that last day, twisting it as he tried to avoid falling on to some wire netting thrown down outside. He limped indoors and Betsy found some clean rag and put a cold compress on the swelling. Joseph, who had seen what happened laughed and their mother said to Daniel, 'You've always been clumsy.'

Betsy was kneeling on the floor tying the cold rag round his ankle and she almost bit her tongue when Daniel shook his head at her to stop her losing her temper and answering back. Later, as they climbed into the trap to leave she said, 'Why do you let her treat you like that?'

'I don't like arguments. But I couldn't leave her to die and Joseph would not have done anything.'

He was silent until they had travelled some distance from Sandilands Farm and then, as though there had been no break in his words he said, 'You heard her, Betsy – what she called me. Joseph and me, we are not full brothers you see. I have always known that.'

'You are her son, no matter who your father was. Did she used to taunt you with that too when you were little, Daniel?'

'Yes. I don't often think about it now and she did feed and clothe me when I was a boy. I still owe her that.' He gave the reins a flick and the pony moved faster.

'You do not owe her anything. She's a cruel, cruel woman and I hate her for what she did to you. What she is still doing to you. Oh Daniel, my love, if I had known all that I would not have lifted a finger to help her.'

She leaned against him and he said quietly, 'Careful, you'll tip us out. It's over now. I should not have mentioned it, so we won't talk of it again.'

For the rest of the journey Betsy thought about the cruelty and ignorance in the world and renewed her determination to do something about it. Teaching folk to read and write was the first step. More and more she realized how lucky she had been. Looking across to Daniel's set face as he drove along, she knew that good did some-times come from bad practices. She would always think that selling people was wicked, but in her case it had proved to be a blessing, even though she still felt ashamed to have had to stand in that line in the market and be looked over like livestock.

As they reached Redwood Farm they saw two of their pigs wandering down the road with Jim herding them back inside. Daniel stopped and climbed down, limping along to help.

'I was milking the cows when I thought I heard someone,' Jim said. 'When I finished I checked. The gate was open and the pigs were out. I'm sure someone was about but whoever it was had gone by the time I came out.'

'Never mind, Jim,' Betsy said. 'Come and have a stoop of ale now everything is safe again.' Looking across to her husband's tired face she added, 'And you need to rest that ankle Daniel.' She took hold of his hand as the three of them went indoors. She pushed away the immediate thought that Thomas Shooter had returned and let the pigs out as revenge for her spurning of him. Was he in the area again and was this the start of a spiteful campaign against them? She shivered and decided to keep an eye on everything even more than usual.

That night as they almost fell into bed and into each other's arms, she was laughing and crying together. Coping with Daniel's surly mother and fending off his brother while running their household for a few days had made her appreciate even more the joy of their own home. She said no more to

Daniel about the way his mother treated him and Joseph. Even if he accepted it and tried to please her, she never would for his sake. Maybe it isn't only women who need to be set free, she thought, but I cannot discuss that with Daniel because I know it would hurt him too much.

Snow fell on Christmas Eve and as Daniel piled more logs on to the fire and Dumbo came to rub against her legs before settling in front of the blaze Betsy thought she must be the happiest woman in the land. All her preparations were done ready for tomorrow's festive meal and she even dared to wonder if 1822 would bring them the child they both hoped for.

'Young Tom who worked here last year is back,' Daniel said coming into the kitchen one morning the following April. Betsy shivered but her husband had his back to her at that point and didn't notice.

'He'll be over the stable again. If you get time slip over with some sheets and bits and pieces so he can be comfortable there, will you?'

As he went through the door Betsy found her voice. 'Where is he now, Daniel?'

'Down the bottom field. He can eat with us at midday, and fend for himself in the evening.' Then he was gone and Betsy shivered again.

She quickly gathered the things she needed and hurried over while she knew Thomas Shooter was a long way away, but his words from a twelvemonth ago as he left the farm pounded in her head. 'You'll pay for this.'

She knew she ought to tell Daniel and the problem would be solved. Yet surely she could handle the trouble herself. If she complained to Daniel now he would wonder why she had not done so last year. She must simply never let a situation arise when she was alone with Tom.

He greeted her with a grin when he came to the table at midday, but said nothing to her. Nevertheless she was conscious that he was watching her throughout the meal and she felt very uncomfortable and glad when the ordeal was over and the men returned to work.

In spite of her optimism at Christmas, she had, since the last miscarriage, been afraid to hope too much that one day she might carry Daniel's child to full term. Daniel said that the next time she must rest from the moment they knew but although she had not argued with him about this, she knew it wasn't the answer. The cause, in her view, still lay within her family background and she was determined to find out much more about the Choicelys. She wasn't sure how she would do this, but her mind constantly reverted to Mrs Wallasey and her many wise words during the years she had worked for her.

'There is always a way,' she had told Betsy on more than one occasion. 'When a difficulty stands between your dream and the reality, examine your dream and if it is genuine then look for another route around the problem.'

'My dream is genuine,' she told Dumbo as he rubbed round her legs one morning when she was working about the house. 'But I don't know how to find the answer without upsetting Daniel.'

The cat moved away, curled his tail around his body and sat as still as the china-cat ornaments offered for sale in the market-place. Betsy smiled down at him, 'You have a lot of patience, Dumbo,' she said, 'but not much intelligence, I'm afraid. It's all instinct with you.'

She had no more trouble with Thomas Shooter. She only saw him when he came to eat in the kitchen and to her great relief he ignored her, never lingering now but going back to the fields with the others. She was glad she hadn't made a fuss because they needed all the help they could get at this time of year and it could be difficult to find anyone else now.

For those first few days after his return she

was anxious in case he pulled the trick of coming over faint 'queer' as he put it, and not returning to the stable loft, but coming into the kitchen instead, but it didn't happen and she felt herself relaxing more. Nevertheless she stayed well away from the stable.

It looked like being a good harvest but Betsy tried to think of an excuse not to attend the harvest supper when the time came, yet if she stayed home that could present an even greater danger. Perhaps it would be best to take part but to stick by Daniel's side throughout the entire evening. These thoughts went round in her head as she busied herself with her daily tasks, until the morning towards the end of harvesting when she saw from the kitchen window her husband and Tom approaching the farm-house.

Tom went round the corner to the stable and Daniel came into the house. 'Bit early for food,' he said, 'but I want to talk to you while the others aren't here.'

Wiping her hands she turned towards him, and he pulled a chair out for her to sit on. 'I'm thinking of taking young Tom on permanently, Betsy. We can afford it and it will mean you won't need to work so hard outside. I know it's a strange time to do this but there's a lot of maintenance work to do around the farm and he can do all this

131

during the next few months.'

At first she didn't fully take in what he was saying, then she felt herself gripping the sides of the chair as his meaning crept into her brain.

'No,' she said, then, grabbing at his hand, 'No, Daniel, please, please don't do that.'

'Why not? He's a good worker and–'

'I can't explain but please don't do it.' He was gazing at her now and quickly she added, 'It's – it's just something I feel. He's not good for the farm – I just know it, Daniel. Please.'

Her husband's face looked grim. 'I'm partly doing it for you. I thought you'd be happy. You won't be toiling in the fields if we take on another hand.'

His expression softened and he put an arm round her shoulders, 'Betsy, I love you and I want the best for you. Someday you'll have the children we both want and it will be better for you not to have to work so hard on the farm. Probably won't need to work in the fields at all. Tom has proved his worth – the fact that he returned this year – after all, he could have picked up casual jobs almost anywhere, but he chose to come back here. Anyway, unless you can find a proper reason not to I shall take him on.' He let his hand slip from her shoulder and she took it in hers, and pressed it close to her heart.

'Please, I beg of you Daniel, don't do this...' She saw Tom come into the kitchen, saw the satisfied smirk on his face and stifled the scream that threatened to erupt. Daniel turned towards the door and motioned Tom to sit at the already laid-up table. Jim arrived at that moment and they all sat down to eat.

Betsy thought she wouldn't be able to swallow a mouthful, but when she noticed Tom glance in her direction she took a large wedge of cheese and put it on her plate. She would not let him see how rattled she was, but her determination to stand out against this proposal at all costs soared. If necessary she would have to confide to Daniel what had happened, and although she knew the hired hand would deny it, Daniel would believe her. Of course he would. The tiny seed of anxiety that he would question why she hadn't told him before was firmly squashed as she stared boldly across the table at Thomas Shooter.

Daniel stayed behind when the two other men left for the fields. 'Now,' he said, 'what is all this nonsense about, Betsy?'

'I don't like Tom Shooter.'

'You won't have to work with him. You will only see him for a short time for his meals. He's a strong lad and–'

'No,' she said, 'no, Daniel. There's something nasty about him.'

'You'll have to come up with more than that.'

'He – he tried to kiss me at the harvest supper last year.'

Daniel said, 'The devil he did. I won't take him on. Why didn't you tell me before?'

'He was leaving the next day and I didn't want to worry you.' When her husband left the kitchen to return to work Betsy sat down quickly. Her heart seemed to be racing around inside her. She put her arms on the table and rested her head on them for a few moments. This always calmed her when she felt really churned up.

Her relief at how easy it had been after all made her feel light-headed. She realized that she was worried about how Daniel would react. His sudden surges of temper never lasted long, but when they happened they were like an explosion and this time she knew she had no right to fly back at him as she usually did.

She stood up and moved across the kitchen. There was much to do for the supper tonight when all the farms in the area joined together for their thanksgiving for the harvest. There was no time to dwell on her joy that by this time tomorrow Tom Shooter would be on his way, never to return to Redwood Farm.

Occasionally Betsy saw the farmer's wives and some of the children at market but she did not know them well. A lot of the wives were older than she was but she did not look for their friendship as she would have done had she been able to go to market during her time with George Hatton. Now she had a busy and fulfilling life, apart from her childlessness. And that was of more concern to her than to Daniel, for she longed to have a family with him. However many children there were she knew he would support her in giving them all, boys or girls, as good an education as they could.

The local farmers all came to Redwood for the celebrations. 'We have one of the largest barns round here,' Daniel had told her before her first harvest supper, 'but everyone brings their share and more.'

Betsy had been baking for days, as had the other farmers' wives in the area, and the dairymaid Hannah had been helping. By that evening the trestle-tables set out in the big barn were groaning with food.

Coming down the lane, many carrying yet more food, were several neighbours and their workers, led by the parson and the fiddler. She had heard that the parson allowed his church to be used as a store for the smugglers who operated around the Kent and Sussex coasts. Most of it was taken on from the church crypt to London and other parts of the country, but some found its way to the rich houses outside the village. The parson was a round-faced, cheery man who preached his sermons each Sunday in a booming voice which dared anyone to go to sleep. 'He is a good man,' Daniel said when they had talked of it one evening while they were sitting comfortably together in the soft glow of the candlelight. 'He would harm no man or beast and he is trusted by all.' Betsy smiled as she remembered again Mrs Wallasey's words to her: *There is always a way, Betsy, always a way.*

It was a jolly procession that wended its way over the fields to Redwood and if it had not been for the prospect that Tom Shooter would be present Betsy would have looked forward to the evening. As it was she wished only for it to be over and for Tom to leave the area for good. Daniel had told her before they went that the farm worker would be off tomorrow morning.

'He can have his share of the fruits of his labour tonight at the supper. I would not send a man away hungry,' he said, 'but he will not be working here again ever.'

He had not yet told the lad but at the harvest supper that evening Daniel said quietly, 'Tom, I won't be taking on anyone else just now. I thought about it when I talked to you, but–'

'Not taking...' Thomas Shooter's eyes narrowed and he moved closer to the farmer. 'You talked it over with *her*, didn't you?' His voice lost the friendly note it usually had when talking to his employer. 'I'm surprised a man would even *mention* it to his woman. But then of course she isn't *only* yours, is she?'

'What do you mean?' They were standing outside the barn, a little away from the merriment going on inside.

Tom shrugged, 'She likes a bit of rough and tumble. You can't watch her all the time. I suppose she thinks you'd find out what we were up to if I was here for more than a few weeks.'

He didn't see the blow coming as Daniel's fist hit him, and when he staggered away to his bed a short while afterwards, nursing his bruises, he vowed he would get even with her. 'Vile bitch,' he muttered, holding his jaw. 'You'll really pay for it this time, you'll see.'

The following morning he collected his wages and left the farm.

At first Daniel didn't believe Tom Shooter's accusations about Betsy but as he worked in the fields and among the animals he knew the opportunities had been there. He remembered when Tom was ill last year and he had sent him to rest. Had he not gone to the stable but to Betsy. Or had she gone to the loft to be with him?

An image of the lad, tall, lithe and athletic,

refused to go away. He never doubted that it would have been Tom who made the first move, but if she had been tempted and succumbed, even just once, then that would explain her fright that it could happen again if Tom stayed. In despair Daniel let the thoughts chase each other round in his head until he knew he must talk to her about it again. He did so that evening. They were sitting opposite each other in the two armchairs and she was fondling Dumbo who, as usual was lying at her feet.

'When Tom Shooter tried to kiss you, Betsy,' he said hesitantly, 'why didn't you scream and make a fuss and – and tell me.'

She stopped stroking the cat and sat upright and very still in the chair.

'You were too far away to hear a scream and I thought I could handle him.'

'How many times did this happen?' He too was still now, but it was a stillness on the verge of eruption. His question surprised her and, seeing the pained expression in his eyes she diluted the truth. 'Only once, Daniel.'

'And you – you didn't...' He stopped and she looked across the short distance between the armchairs and stared into his face.

'How could you even think ... Of *course* I didn't. Don't you believe me?' Her voice shook with anger and emotion.

He went across to her and took her hands

in his. 'You didn't want him here from the start this season but I thought it would make it easier for you and I played into his hands. If only I'd known.' His grip tightened and she leant forward and kissed him.

There was wonder in his eyes too, now. 'Forgive me Betsy. I'm not blaming you. I love you so much and I'm jealous.' That night she lay awake long after Daniel was asleep and snoring. It was over; Tom Shooter had gone for good this time. He wouldn't ever seek work here again after the pounding Daniel had given him.

She took no pleasure in men fighting over her and she tried to put the ordeal of the last few weeks out of her mind but sleep wouldn't come. In the morning she was bleary-eyed and irritable.

Daniel stamped off to work, saying, 'Whatever's got into you, I want it out by the time I return. You may be beautiful but you're bad-tempered too.' He looked up at the straw halter as he went by, or it seemed to her he did. When he had gone she burst into tears. Even Dumbo wasn't around to comfort her, and eventually she stood up and began clearing the breakfast-table.

Half-way through the morning, just when she had put some pies in the kitchen range, there was a tap at the back door. She opened it to find a gypsy woman standing there.

'You buy some lucky heather?' She thrust

a tiny posy of white heather at Betsy. 'My, you're a very unhappy lady,' the gypsy said, 'you have big trouble.'

Betsy bought the heather, six bunches of it, and the gypsy said, 'I see great happiness for you but trouble first.'

'What kind of trouble?'

Wise old eyes gazed at her solemnly. 'With a man. Be careful.' More than that she would not – or maybe could not – say.

Perhaps she was 'seeing' what had already happened, Betsy thought when she returned to her cooking. But now that Tom Shooter had gone surely things would come right with Daniel. Unless there was another man in the future who would seek to come between them. All she could think of was Daniel's brother, Joseph. But even Daniel made sure he was never left alone with her.

She knew she would hate to be ugly and she loved being beautiful but her looks had led to trouble all through her life. At home with her family, at work with the other maids and with the master, and now with the husband she adored.

She felt certain that she had inherited them from her father's family and wished so much that she could find out who he was. There was no doubt in her mind that she had been told lies about her beginnings and that the older generation knew the story. Her siblings probably copied the attitude of their elders, as Daniel had suggested.

She certainly didn't look like Sir Richard Choicely, but maybe her father was a cousin or nephew, or brother even. She paused as her hand reached for the flour again. Did Richard Choicely have any brothers? There were two sons but no mention of brothers or sisters in the facts they had unearthed about the family. Did Sir Benjamin Choicely have other sons than Richard – younger ones, one of whom might be her father? Sir Benjamin may have had brothers whose sons surname would be the same.

When Daniel returned he seemed in a brighter mood and commented on the delicious smell of home cooking. Jim too smiled at her and said how good it smelt.

'I've made more than one pie,' she told him, 'so you can take one home with you.'

'Thanks, missus.' He sat quietly at the table as usual and she sighed with relief that at least there was one here whom she had no need to fear. Jim was a good worker and knew his place.

Chapter 7

'This'll do.' Thomas Shooter jumped from the wagon, shouted a brief thanks over his shoulder and set off to walk the rest of the way to Redwood Farm. As he walked he whistled and a strange, grim-looking expression, half smile, half sneer, hovered round his mouth. Only a few more hours and he would have his revenge on them. Especially on her. He felt the excitement rising in his groin. It was revenge with a bonus because he meant to have her too.

When Daniel found out what was going on, or what appeared to be going on, he could guess the reaction and he would make sure *she* stayed in the loft. Then he would have her, and afterwards he would spit on her before he left for ever. There were two important things in his life, women and work. He had no trouble finding either. He loved working on the farms, and although he could not have put it into words he felt at one with the land as he toiled in the fields. Women were his other passion, but not *any* women. They had to be of his choosing. He had power in both situations and it felt good.

He swung jauntily along but stopped

whistling as he neared the lane where the farm was. His plan would only work if he was not seen or heard.

He had travelled the same road only two days ago, when he had sought out one of the boys from the village three miles from the hamlet where the farm was. From his time in the area he knew this particular lad was a bit simple but would do anything for money. As far as Tom knew the boy never spent it, unless he went to the fair once a year, but he hoarded every copper as a miser hoards his gold.

He told him exactly what he wanted him to do and the boy repeated it several times to make sure he had got it right.

'But not a word to anyone,' Tom warned, 'because if you do I will know and I will slit you from here to here.' He drew an imaginary line from the top of the lad's head through to his feet. 'It will be the most painful death for you if you breathe a word to anyone. You do *not* know me, you have never seen me before, you are a simpleton who doesn't understand what he is saying or doing. *Understand?*'

The boy nodded quickly and many times. He understood only too well.

'Before I kill you I will cut out your tongue, so be sure you do exactly as I say. If you do then nothing bad will ever happen to you.'

'Y-yes.' The village lad's voice was little above a whisper as he shied away from Tom.

He was there, crouched down by the hedge, when Tom arrived. 'Anyone see you?' Tom hissed at him.

'N-no one.'

'You sure?' Tom gripped the yoke of his smock and once more the boy nodded. Tom dived his hand into his pocket and produced a coin.

'What are you going to tell him. Come on, spit it out?'

'Master, there's someone trying to get in the hayloft.'

'That's right. *Make* him come. Keep saying it if he doesn't come the first time. Then what do you do?'

'Go across to the kitchen and tell missus master is in hayloft and hurt.'

'Good. Then run off and wait for me in the village.' He took another coin from his pocket and held it in front of the boy, 'I'll give you this other one then. Go on, run now.'

The boy looked at him for a moment, then set off for the field where Daniel was. His lolloping half-run and half-walk was surprisingly fast and a grin of excitement spread across his features as he went. All the while he was saying out loud the words he had been practising, 'Master, there's someone trying to get in the hayloft.' 'Missus,

144

master is in hayloft and hurt.'

Thomas Shooter glanced towards the kitchen door before sneaking into the hayloft. He thought she would be in the kitchen or dairy and he also knew she would rush to the hayloft as soon as the boy told her that Daniel was there and injured. He had to take a chance the boy would be fast enough, but he thought he would. It was his natural instinct to run from people rather than linger and by the time Daniel had the message and reached the hayloft Betsy would be there. She only had to come across the yard after all.

He knew the mattress would be there in its usual place. Swiftly he took sheets from his bag and spread them untidily on the lumpy mattress they kept there for the casual labourer. He felt the hot blood rushing through his body as he rumpled them into disorder. Timing was everything, although if she arrived before Daniel he could hold her there. She would scream and fight him though so he needed to have her trapped in the hayloft without her realizing he was there. They thought he was such a simple soul but he would show them.

He went into the dark recess at the back, divested himself of all his clothes, then wrapped his smock around him without putting it on. With growing excitement he waited. The timing was perfect. He heard Betsy rush in, calling her husband's name and within a couple of seconds Daniel was there. Thomas Shooter threw off the garment covering his nakedness and came from behind the shelf to confront them.

Betsy screamed and turned into her husband's arms, while Tom advanced towards her. 'You said he would be away all day,' he shouted, his voice aggrieved and accusing. Thrusting Betsy from him Daniel struck the first blow, but although he took the younger man by surprise with that one, Tom had the advantage of height and strength.

It was over in minutes, and while Daniel lay winded on the floor, Tom hauled Betsy from her husband's side and dragged her through to where he had been hiding before either of them arrived.

'I'll give you something to remember me by,' he said exultantly. 'Here.' Before he could wrestle her to the ground her foot found its target and Thomas Shooter was writhing in agony on the floor. Daniel was staggering to his feet as she returned to his side. His face was bloodied and one eye almost closed. Roughly he pushed her aside and zigzagged towards Tom. 'Get out,' he said.

In vain Betsy protested her innocence. Daniel stormed around the farm grim-

146

lipped and silent. She couldn't bear the hurt that showed in his eyes, in his walk, in his whole stance. Yet she knew she couldn't assuage it unless he believed in her and this was the one thing he would not do.

'Daniel, it was a trick, can't you see that?' she begged, *'I did not know he was there–'*

'Don't make excuses, Betsy. You were tempted and – and I can even understand it, but stop lying to me.'

'I'm not, I'm not. For pity's sake, Daniel you must believe me. I tell you, I promise you, that I did not know he was there. This boy came and told me you were in the hayloft and injured and I rushed over. I don't know what happened next. You came in and – and suddenly Tom was there with no clothes on...' She sank into a chair and sobbed, not even hearing her husband walk out of the room.

She woke in the night to find herself crying uncontrollably and Daniel as far over on the opposite side of the bed as he could possibly get without falling off the edge. In an effort to subdue the sobs she rammed her fist into her mouth and buried her head beneath the pillow. A few moments later she felt Daniel's arm come round her, then the pillow moved and wordlessly he embraced her.

'Daniel, Daniel, my love I'm so sorry,' she said as soon as she could speak coherently.

He moved away slightly and she took hold of his hand and put it against her breast.

'Stop it,' he shouted, his voice hoarse with emotion. 'Is that what you did to him? How many times? Very convenient, wasn't it? Me down in the furthest field, unsuspecting. How many times has he been over here? How many times has he looked in to see if the coast was clear during these last months? No wonder you didn't want him here all the time, I might have realized what was going on, mightn't I? This way you could have it all, your lover and your security. Well it's over now. When the fair comes in a few days' time you'll be there, standing in line again. Yes, you will.' His grip on her tightened. 'All your fine talk of men and women being equal. They aren't equal, they never will be equal because women lure men on until they trust them, then they do the dirty on them. I was the biggest fool not to realize...' Suddenly he went from the bed and grabbing his pillow said, 'I'll sleep on the sofa tonight and you had better pack your things ready for the fair the day after tomorrow.'

Betsy sat up in bed after he'd gone, shaking all over, the tears in her eyes spent for the moment, the ones in her heart trembling to be let loose. Surely he didn't mean that? Surely it was said in the turmoil of what was happening? She drew her knees up as though in physical pain and as her head came forward on to them so the tears began to flow again. This time she did not try to stop them. She couldn't remember falling back on to her pillow and sleeping but at some point during the night she must have done so because she woke and for a second wondered why she felt so bloated and awful. The memory of yesterday hit her and she hastily washed, dressed and went downstairs.

There was no sign of Daniel but the crockery on the table indicated that he had eaten and drunk. Suddenly she knew what she must do. Find that boy, the one who had rushed in and told her Daniel was in the hayloft and injured. Who was he? Where had he come from? She didn't recall ever seeing him before.

There was no possibility that Daniel would tell her if he knew him; her tears threatened again and angrily she brushed them away. She must *think*, must keep her mind clear because something was terribly wrong. Why had Daniel come to the hayloft then? What had brought him racing up the steps? Had the boy told him she was lying injured in there, too? It all led to one thought – that the despicable Thomas Shooter was behind it and had brought the boy with him to put his plan into action.

In her mind she heard his words from that last harvest supper. *You'll pay for this,* and she was sure now that that had been no idle threat. Yet how could she convince her beloved Daniel that things were not as they had appeared. That she had had no idea Tom Shooter was anywhere near the place when she rushed over there. Oh, it was clever, no doubt about that. But worst of all, it had succeeded. Daniel had believed him.

Wearily she poured herself a drink, then began to clear up and prepare a meal. This afternoon she would walk into the village and try to find the boy, although in her heart she felt sure he didn't live there. He was someone Tom brought with him just for that purpose. Yet he had to have come from somewhere, and he didn't live nearby or she would know him. The village of Graceden was the next obvious place because she really couldn't imagine Thomas Shooter having a young boy tagging along with him on his travels. So maybe, just maybe he was from this area. If he was she would find him and get to the truth of the matter.

Later, over in the dairy with Hannah, she did all the necessary work, and not once during that long morning did she catch a glimpse of her husband.

Daniel and Jim came in together at midday and although Daniel spoke to her when he could not easily avoid doing so, the atmosphere was as heavy as the bruises on his eye and cheekbone. She longed to bathe them, kiss them, cradle his dear head against her, but she dared not do any of these things now. As usual Jim didn't linger, and today neither did Daniel. As he went through the door close on the cowman's heels he did just glance her way, though, and the look in his eyes and on his face showed her that he was suffering as she was.

That afternoon she walked the three miles to the village, trying all the while to recall what the boy had looked like. She really hadn't taken much notice of him but she thought he was about ten years old. He had gabbled the message about Daniel being injured and she had not even thought about who he was, where he had come from, or how he had known. She had simply rushed over to the stable, as Tom Shooter had known she would, of course.

If only she could talk to Daniel and get him to see this too, that they had been tricked, both of them. But then Daniel had not known about the scene in the kitchen when Tom Shooter came out from the larder where he had lain in wait for her. She couldn't tell him now. It would only make things worse – as if the situation could be any worse.

She had to find that boy and bring him back to tell Daniel he had been telling lies, that Thomas Shooter had hired him to do just that. Everything hinged on finding him and she had no idea where to begin. It was a small community and surely someone would know him if he lived there, but if, as she now strongly suspected, Tom had brought him from another place there would be nothing she could do.

As she approached the first house in the village she fingered the gold locket that Daniel had bought her and which she always wore around her neck. 'Please, please, let me find the boy,' she murmured to God.

Richard Choicely saw Betsy as he rode through the village where he was visiting an old retainer. She was walking. He reigned in his horse and spoke to her. 'Good afternoon, Mistress Forrester, it is a pleasure to see you again.'

Flustered, Betsy dropped a curtsy and he said curtly, 'There is no need for that.' He dismounted and stood by her side, holding the horse's reins loosely. 'I see we are both on errands in the same village. I trust you and your husband are well?'

'Thank you, yes we are.' Then, because she did not know what to say next she added, 'I am looking for a young boy, about ten years of age.'

Startled, Richard said, 'Then may I escort you to his house, Mistress Forrester?'

'I – er, I am not sure which is his house, Sir Richard.'

Richard glanced around, 'What is his name?'

'I do not know that either.'

'But you are sure he lives here?'

Her beautiful face was solemn, sadness showed in her eyes, he saw now, as she said, 'I do not know where he lives, but I believe it could be in this place.'

Richard was puzzled. There was something strange going on here. Why would the farmer's wife be on her own seeking a young lad whose name she did not know. Or even if he resided here. She must be several miles from the farm, yet she appeared to have walked in for no other purpose than to find someone she was not even sure lived here.

'Well,' he said, 'I happen to know somebody who was born and bred in this place. He is an old man now but he used to work for me. He will certainly know of all the young people in the village. Would you like to talk to him? He may be able to tell you where to find the lad you are seeking.'

Her smile set his blood racing. 'I would, Sir Richard. You are most kind.'

'Not at all, it will be a pleasure.'

Walking with her he led the horse and together they went down the village street until they came to Lilac Cottage. Sir Richard tethered the horse to a post.

'This way,' he said as he walked along the narrow path to the front door. The old man who let them in was bent and his face wrinkled and weather-beaten. Richard introduced him as Sam.

'Sam worked at Chasebury for many years but he was born here in this village and knows everyone, eh Sam? This lady is looking for a young boy – how old did you say he was, Mistress Forrester?'

'About ten I think.' She was grateful not to be asked why she wanted him. It would be difficult to explain.

'There are one or two lads around that age here. 'Tis not a big place,' Sam said. 'What does he look like, this boy?'

Betsy decided to be totally honest. 'I only caught a glimpse of him,' she said, 'when he delivered a message to our farm. I didn't take much notice of his features really, but I do not think he was very tall...' she glanced towards Sir Richard, who smiled encouragingly at her.

'Can you recall whether he was dark or fair or had anything outstanding about him – maybe a limp, or an accent – that would possibly help.'

'I'm sorry I can't. Oh, he didn't limp because he ran quite fast.'

Sam said, 'Well, there's only about three or four that fit, unless you count young Zac. He's a bit simple, though. Where is your farm?'

'It's three miles from here. I'm not certain

that the boy lives here,' she added truthfully, addressing Sam. She knew she was on a bit of a wild-goose chase because the more she thought about it, the more sure she became that Tom had brought the lad with him, maybe from his last employment. It was the most likely explanation.

'Well, he must live somewhere,' Richard said, 'unless he roughs it in the woods.' He wanted to ask her what the message was about, to find some clue as to why she needed to find this boy. Why had she and not her husband come on this quest, why was she on foot instead of in the trap? Not wishing to embarrass her in front of Sam, he said quietly to him, 'If you could tell us where they all live perhaps we shall find him.'

Sam gave directions to each of the cottages and farms where the boys could be located; there were five of them, two were brothers, 'and Zac – he's about twelve now I think, but he's not big and could be mistaken for younger. He does roam about a bit – strange boy. The others used to mock him when he was younger because he's not all there y'know. Not his fault, but he shies away from people and I wouldn't think he'd be delivering messages. Goes around on his own, usually clutching an old tin. I asked him once what was in it and he looked wild then and rushed off rattling it as he went.

Sounded like a lot of stones in there.'

As she left to try the places Sam suggested, Richard came to the door with her. 'I shall be here for thirty minutes or so,' he said, 'if you should need any assistance.'

She thanked him, and set off down the village street. The first two cottages were close together but neither of the boys living there had delivered a message anywhere recently. The next place was a small farm and this was where the brothers lived with their parents. It took longer to find anyone there, but she did eventually come across the farmer's wife who assured her that both boys were busy on the farm every spare moment they had and certainly hadn't been out of the village since last fair-day.

That only left the one called Zac, and the lad who came to their kitchen door that fateful day had not seemed simple. He had talked quickly and rushed away, but in her memory now he was just a blur; her mind had been full of Daniel lying injured in the hayloft. If only she had asked his name or – no, she told herself, he didn't come from here, it didn't make sense. Much more likely that Tom Shooter had picked him up on his travels and somehow got the lad to do his dirty work for him.

She reached the cottage which was at the far end of the village – the very last one in fact, for after that were open fields. At first there was no reply to her knock, but as she was turning away she heard a movement. Suddenly the boy appeared from round the back and raced in a strangely lolloping fashion straight past her and across the fields. He was going very fast and she knew he was the same boy she had seen yesterday.

In the far distance she could see a man; she presumed him to be his father, and as the lad's figure grew smaller she knew she would never catch him. But she knew now where he lived, she even knew his name, Zac, and ... but would he own up? He was simple, Sam had said. A figure of fun, maybe no one would believe him if he did tell the truth: that Thomas Shooter had forced him to give that lying message to them both so he could trick them and have his revenge.

With a deep sigh she made her way back down the village street. Sir Richard was waiting for her at Sam's gate.

'Did you find him?' he asked.

'I'm not sure. I think it was the one called Zac, but he ran off across the fields before I had a chance to speak to him.'

'Is it very important that you speak to him?' Sir Richard's voice was quiet and gentle and almost had her in tears because he was bothering.

'No, no I suppose not,' she said. 'I must go now. Thank you for your help, Sir Richard.'

He reached as though to take hold of her hands, then, not wishing to compromise her, he knew well enough how many people would be watching from their windows, he let his hands fall to his side as he said, 'Richard please, and may I call you Betsy? I know it is your name.'

'Yes, please do.'

'If only I had brought the carriage instead of a horse today I could have taken you home. It is a goodly walk.'

'Thank you,' she said, 'but I shall enjoy the walk. Good-day.' She hesitated for a second before adding, 'Richard.'

'Good-day, Betsy. My regards to your husband.' He watched until she was out of sight, then mounted his horse for the ride back to Chasebury.

Daniel came into the farmhouse kitchen late in the afternoon. There was no sign of Betsy and no evidence of a meal cooking. Looking round he realized the whole place seemed silent and empty. He went into the other downstairs rooms but although everything was neat and tidy she wasn't there. Alarmed now he raced upstairs, almost tripping over Dumbo who was lying down outside the bedroom door. He burst in but there was nobody there. It was the same all over the house. Each time he opened a door he was afraid he might find her lying

158

collapsed on the floor.

'Dumbo, Dumbo, where is she? Where's your mistress?' he asked of the bemused cat. As he hurried across the yard to the stable panic struck him. *Surely not, she won't be there.* He rushed up the steps, the memory of the last time overwhelming him for a few seconds. The hayloft was empty too. He searched the fields, the lane, then in despair returned to the house.

He took the straw halter from the nail and stared at it as if that could conjure up his beloved wife. He knew she hated it, yet it was his assurance that she was his, that she would stay, that legally she belonged to him. 'I'll burn it,' he muttered. 'Just let her come back safe, that's all that matters.' He hung it back on the hook and went to the kitchen. What now – where else could he look? Had she gone off with Tom? He wanted so much to believe her, he *did* believe her, yet how was it that she had been there in the hayloft and Thomas Shooter was there too, naked?

In his mind's eye he saw again the rumpled bed, Betsy looking distraught and bewildered, and then, just a second later, that lad appearing, naked. Tom's words returned and began hammering into his mind: *You said he would be away all day...* He could hear them, smell the desire emanating from him.

Betsy had looked devastated, but only now did he stop to think about why. He had presumed it was because they had been caught, but was it because she was stunned? Remembering her passionate denials now, Daniel let common sense creep into the emotion he felt. Had they been taken in by the lad? Was it a trick to get them both to the hayloft on a false errand. Who was the boy who had dashed up to him and told him that someone was trying to get into the hayloft? That the missus was there?

Betsy had denied any wrongdoing. Said she had not known Thomas Shooter was here, that it was a trick. He must find her, where was she? He loved her so much. He walked back into the hall, took the halter from its hook once more and knew he could never use it again. He had been mad last night when he threatened her with that; angry and hurt, and her sudden apology confused him, but never could he make her stand in the marketplace to be sold. Even if what he had believed was true, and now he doubted that too.

At that moment he saw her. She looked through the window straight at him, standing there with the halter in his hand. Quickly he hung it back on the nail and rushed outside to greet her.

Betsy saw Daniel through the window and

he had the straw halter in his hand. So he meant it, he was planning to take her to the fair. Deep in her heart she still hoped he loved and believed in her. Tired from her trudge to the village and back and the lack of success in finding and bringing the boy with her, tears were not far away. Blinking several times she took a deep breath, drew in her stomach muscles, held her head high and walked indoors. They almost collided but Betsy stepped quickly to one side.

'I couldn't find you. Where have you been?' Daniel said, relief making his voice sound harsher than usual.

'I went to find the boy who lied.'

He looked startled, then reached for her hand. 'Did you find him? How did you know where to look?'

'I found him but he ran away. He lives in the village. I must go and tidy myself and get the meal ready.' Daniel let go of her hand and watched her slowly mount the stairs.

Later that evening, after a fairly silent meal Daniel went into his office saying he had some work to do. Betsy sat in the armchair with the sewing-basket on her lap and Dumbo at her feet. Every so often she reached down and felt his soft fur. She wished she could let him know she loved him and would miss him, but how could you tell a dumb animal such things and make them understand.

Tears welled in her eyes and she knew she needed to rest because her mind was made up. She would not stay and be taken to the fair and sold again. That Daniel could even think of it appalled her and she shut her mind to it. She needed all her wits about her now to avoid this awful thing. There would be plenty of time for tears and memories later, just now she had to be strong and she knew she could only be so if she refused to think about anything except escape and sleep.

When she looked through the open door of the little room where Daniel did his accounts he was sitting at his desk. He wasn't doing anything, simply sitting there looking miserable and it was all she could do not to run in and throw her arms round him.

'Goodnight, Daniel,' she said, then turned and went up the stairs to their bedroom. She would not beg him to try again with their marriage, but she also had no intention of being taken to the fair. Anything but that. Every bone in her body and every feeling in her heart and mind seemed to ache and she knew she needed to rest now so she could prepare herself tomorrow, because the day after that the fair began.

Chapter 8

Betsy was up early the following morning. Daniel sat down for his breakfast with scarcely a word and even Dumbo slunk outside much earlier than usual. Poor cat, she thought, this terrible atmosphere is even affecting him.

As soon as he finished eating Daniel pushed his chair back and went out, briefly touching her shoulder as he passed her chair. 'Got to get on, a lot to do today,' he said.

She sat for a moment finishing her drink and trying not to think of what the future held for either of them. Then she rose and went outside to wash the dishes. Back indoors she swept the kitchen before going upstairs to the bedroom. She put clean sheets on the bed and bundled the others into the tub along with towels and clothes. She wanted to leave everything as up to the minute as possible.

Downstairs again she worked in the dairy until noon then prepared the table with bread, cheese and pickle. She watched Daniel and Jim eating heartily but had little appetite herself. When they had returned to work she began preparing the evening meal for herself and Daniel. When all was ready to cook she went upstairs again and packed her bag.

She took nothing except what she had arrived with, the gold locket Daniel had bought her, and what she had left of the housekeeping money to tide her over until she found a job. She could turn her hand to most things and there would be potential employers at the fair. She might even end up as a scullery-maid again, but only as a last resort, she thought. There were better jobs than that for someone who could read and write.

If only her special lady, Mrs Wallasey was still alive. For the first time that day she smiled to herself. If Mrs Wallasey *had* been alive this situation would never have arisen. But then she would not have known Daniel and in spite of the dreadful happenings of these last few days she would not wish to go back to a time when she didn't know and love her husband.

The halter was back on the hook but she couldn't forget that Daniel had had it in his hands when she returned. His words from the other evening haunted her: *It's over. When the fair comes you'll be there...*

In bed that night when he had suddenly rolled over to comfort her, she had tried to explain but even in her misery she could see how hard it was for him to believe. She hated Thomas Shooter and he seemed to be winning. For a few hours she had thought the boy Zac would be able to put things right between herself and Daniel. That she had found him was a miracle but there her luck had run out. She did at least know where he was now, but with such a strange boy as he obviously was there was no guarantee that he would tell the truth about what happened.

In her own mind she was clear that Tom had planned this. He must have bribed that boy to bring the messages but, confronted with the scene as they both were, Daniel could not be expected to believe that nothing was going on, she thought. Her amazement returned afresh as, for the first time since it had happened, she pictured herself rushing in and looking round for her husband, then his voice calling her and his distraught expression, and Thomas Shooter's naked appearance, all within a few seconds. It still seemed impossible that their lives could be turned inside out so fast and frighteningly.

The only clear thought in her head was that she would not be sold again. She would rather starve. She hesitated over taking money with her, then reasoned that she would need it to survive until she found work. Whenever she had anything left from the housekeeping Daniel gave her each week she had kept it in the corner of the drawer where her underwear was. It wasn't a lot but she had been saving it to buy Daniel a present. Now she took it out and tied it into her handkerchief. Her need was the greater now and she was thankful she had it.

That night they lay side by side but not touching in the big double bed. She felt Daniel stir every so often and once he gave a great sigh. She waited for him to turn to her, but instead he turned the other way and soon appeared to be asleep. She lay still beside him, remembering, in spite of herself, that first night when he had been out for hours helping his neighbour with the calving. They had lain together then and she had been grateful that he wanted nothing more. Now she longed for him suddenly to take her in his arms and make love to her. The realistic side of her knew that was no longer likely to happen and she closed her eyes in the hope that sleep would come to block out her memories for a while.

Betsy rose a little after four o clock, she had slept fitfully. She crept about and when she was ready to leave she went to the kitchen and set the crockery out for Daniel's breakfast. She took some bread and cheese for herself, put on her cloak, took up her bundle and slipped quietly out of the house.

She did not take the main road, which she

knew Daniel would use later, but instead went across the fields once she was clear of the farmhouse. As long as she headed in the right direction she would stand less chance of being apprehended. She knew she needed to return to the track at some point, but by then Daniel would be a long way in front of her in the horse and cart.

She did not expect to reach the fair until tomorrow, and she might even find work somewhere on the way and not need to go there at all. She went at a reasonable pace, while not rushing too much, and every hour or so she sat down to rest. She saw no one but a shepherd in the distance until she climbed a stile and found herself in a lane. About twenty minutes later a farm-cart came alongside her.

'You be making for the fair?'

'Yes, I am.'

'Hoist yerself up then, I be going there.'

The speaker was clad in a buff-coloured smock and as soon as she was in the cart he set off again. Two hours later they reached the fair.

Betsy jumped from the cart and thanked the farmer for the ride. 'I'm looking for work,' she said. 'Do you know of any here-abouts?'

'Can't say as I do.' He looked at her specu-latively, 'Hmm, shouldn't think you'll have much trouble, a comely wench like you.'

Betsy made for the marshal's office, and settled herself in the shadows to watch, fascinated as the fair came to life. Some folk had arrived overnight and were busy setting out their stalls. Almost everything anyone could want was available here. It wasn't a hiring-fair, but a general one, although hiring did go on. The only area she wanted to avoid was the wife-selling – but she was watching with the crowd when the marshal made his opening proclamation. She was fairly certain that Daniel would not have arrived so soon, but just in case she stood behind a man of large proportions so that she was well hidden from the view of anyone standing opposite or nearby.

The marshal was a giant of a man, resplendent in velvet. His voice carried across the vast heath as he declared that they must all 'keep the peace, that no manner of victual you sell be other than good and wholesome, that no manner of persons may buy or sell but with true weights and measures sealed according to statute. That any person who is injured or wronged by any other person at the fair must come with complaint before the steward.' In conclusion he said, 'Therefore now begin in God's name and the King's and God send every man luck and this fair a good continuance.'

Betsy had the bread and cheese she had brought from home, and because she had not had to walk most of the way, as she had expected, she did not feel tired. If she could find work here for the week at the fair, it would give her enough money to travel further if she was unsuccessful in finding something permanent in this area.

She needed a job where she was not on show because Daniel would almost certainly be coming and he mustn't know she was here. But the fair was large enough to lose herself in and she would be watching for him. She did not think she would have difficulty in avoiding a meeting. It was the only way to avoid the fate she dreaded.

When she saw the cattle being herded into place she sought out the man in charge and he took her on. Half-way through the morning one of the women who was also helping offered her some food.

'Thank you, but I have some here.' Betsy opened her bag and brought out some bread.

'We have a caravan over there. You can come there for a while with me to get a bit of peace and quiet if you like,' said the woman. 'My name's Rosalie, but everyone calls me Rosa.'

She was much older than Betsy; her dark-grey hair was neatly braided and her brown eyes seemed to draw Betsy into their warm depths. She wore a simple grey dress but used a bright scarf around her neck almost as a collar.

'Thank you, I should like that,' Betsy said.

Rosa took her to a corner of the field where their caravan was. The woman and her husband travelled to fairs around the country; they were not gypsies, she told Betsy, but they enjoyed the roving life. Both of them were knowledgeable about herbs and flowers, about animals and wild life, but could only read by recognizing words and committing them to memory.

'Words like fair, market, and all the things we need,' Rosa said. 'We can write our name and prices for when we have a stall.' She picked up a bundle of tickets and Betsy saw that the woman's writing was strong. 'I can write most things if I see them in front of me, but lots of people cannot read and we tell them how much.'

'They bargain with us,' Bill said, a smile creasing his weatherbeaten face. 'But Rosa is good at the writing and she likes doing it.'

Betsy looked at her new friend. 'How did you learn, Rosa?'

'I watched and listened.'

'And asked folk,' Bill said, throwing his arm round Rosa's shoulder.

'No one minds if you really want to know,' Rosa said, 'and sometimes I could help them in return.' Noticing Betsy's questioning look she said, 'I sensed *your* unhappiness and knew you had troubles.'

Betsy began to feel better as Rosa's soft voice told her about their travelling life. 'It suits us,' she said. 'We are happy roaming the country together. Now, have you somewhere to stay tonight?'

Betsy admitted she had not. 'I shall curl up under a hedge,' she said, but Rosa raised her hands in horror at the idea.

'There is room for you here, eh, Bill?'

'Of course there is. Now if we all want to keep our employment we ought to get back to work I think.'

As they set off Rosa laid her hands on Betsy's shoulders. 'I cannot see the future,' she said, 'but I can often feel it. It is pushing at me right now and there is much happiness in yours. The colours are dim when seen close to, but in the distance they are shining bright.'

Betsy felt awkward. No one had ever talked to her in this way before. Seeing her embarrassment Rosa laughed softly, 'You can tell me I'm talking nonsense if you like, but remember this when everything is bad for you, Betsy. Now we must hurry.' She led the way, weaving in and out of the crowds until they reached the cattle-stalls. Later Betsy went back for another meal with them and stayed the night in the caravan.

She managed all week by helping with the cattle and making herself as useful as possible, and at the end of each day she was paid. By the end of the week, however, she was still without employment. None of the gentry would take her on, even as the most menial servant. One loud-mouthed bristling 'gentleman' said within her hearing, 'That's the one for me away from the house, just ripe for the picking....'

She had her own back for that when he approached her later. She was washing some of the cattle and threw the bucket of water over him, pretending to the others it had been an accident. He was furious, but by acting simple and demure she had the satisfaction of seeing him the laughing-stock among his cronies.

It was the laughter that drew Daniel over. She saw him approaching and dodged out of sight. Touching the locket, hidden beneath the high neckline of her dress, she wove in and out of the people until she reached Rosa's caravan which was near a hedge. Neither Rosa nor Bill were there and she lingered for a while, hiding alongside it. From there she could see if anyone approached and be ready to dive into the bushes. She was certain Daniel hadn't seen her, and although the sight of him had set her heart racing she was not going to be caught and sold. Never, never, never.

After a short time she returned to the cattle-market. She felt sure that Daniel would have moved away by now and relief flooded through her when she saw she was right. There was no sign of him.

There was a young girl washing the cattle, a girl who had not been there before. As she went forward Betsy was stopped short when the hirer saw her. 'I've got somebody else,' he said. 'Someone who won't turn the place into a rowdy music hall. You keep away from here.'

For once she did not argue. Knowing Daniel was here somewhere she did not wish to draw more attention to herself. Dejectedly she walked away.

Head down and desperately wondering where to try next for work, she almost bumped into Sir Richard Choicely.

'Betsy,' he said, beaming at her. 'How fortunate. I have just been speaking to your husband and he is looking everywhere for you.'

Wildly she glanced round but there was no sign of Daniel. 'Thank you, sir – thank you, Richard, I will go and find him,' she said, and to his astonishment she ran quickly through the crowds away from him.

Chapter 9

When Richard Choicely returned to Chasebury that evening he thought again about
Betsy Forrester. He had been amazed when
she ran off so quickly, almost as though she
were running away from him. She had not
even asked where it was that he had seen her
husband. And she had looked so startled,
almost afraid, he thought. He wondered
whether there was any kind of trouble
between them. Maybe they had quarrelled.
Now that he came to reflect upon it Daniel
Forrester had seemed very agitated.

It was none of his business really, but
Richard was uneasy about his feelings for
Betsy. She excited him physically and at the
same time he felt such a tenderness for her.
She was exquisitely beautiful and while he
longed to make passionate love to her there
was a part of him that wanted to protect her.
In addition to all that he knew that she
could be his niece.

The more he thought about that aspect
the more it seemed likely. The dates fitted
and her resemblance to his mother and to
Ben was extraordinary. She *must* be family.
He poured himself a brandy and decided to

ride over to the Forresters' place the following day and quietly check things out. He would say he had business in the area and, finding himself close to the farm where his steward had been injured, he had called to offer friendly greetings. That it was not a usual procedure, to pay a social call on a farmer and his wife who were not connected to his estate, he shrugged off. Richard had never let his position stand in the way of talking and mixing with people he found interesting. And he found Daniel Forrester and his wife, especially his wife, very interesting indeed.

Something odd was going on. There was, after all, that business of seeing her when he visited Sam and she was looking for a young boy about whom she knew very little. The boy she found and whom she thought was the one she needed was the lad Sam said was a bit simple, called Zac. Where did he fit into all this? It was a strange situation.

Richard also wanted to find out who the woman running from the scene of his brother's accident was. His father's game-keeper was a truthful and honest man, not given to fantasies, and if he told his son about this woman, then she existed and she was up to no good, he thought.

In his mind he went over what Jim Pike, had told him. That his father had seen a rope stretched between two trees but when he returned after they had taken Ben to the house, the rope was gone. And he saw a woman with a black shawl over her head hurrying through the woods.

The most likely suspect was Betsy's mother, but would she have risked being seen so soon afterwards? Or had she had no choice? Maybe she had not expected Ben to be found so quickly and of course if his and Jim Pike the elder's surmising was right, she had to retrieve the rope as quickly as possible. The more he thought about it the more confident he was that Betsy's mother had murdered his brother because none of the family would acknowledge the child.

If he was able to prove that Betsy was Ben's daughter and had Choicely blood in her he might also find that her mother was a murderess. Perhaps he should not take this any further but simply get on with his own life. He knew he would not do that until he had found an answer.

Richard had always wanted to know things ever since he was a child. The coachman had shown him how the wheels were attached, how they turned, how everything was made. The cook had shown him how to make little cakes and biscuits, the butler had explained how wines were made, from the picking of the grapes to the bottling and racking and the housekeeper's daughter had taught him about love. She was in her early twenties and he was seventeen when she took him into the summer-house.

He had never forgotten her and even now could picture her framed in the doorway, pulling down her pink-cotton skirt and smiling at him. 'Thank you Richard,' she had said. 'I'm going to stay with an aunt for a week but I'll see you when I come home.' There had only been one more time with her because she went away soon after and married a farmer. He never saw her again.

What he wanted to know now was more difficult than any of the things that had gone before. Maybe too much time had elapsed to unearth the truth but he was going to try.

Daniel scoured the fair for Betsy. Several times he caught a glimpse of dark hair, which was always someone else. He talked to people everywhere, a laughing man in the crowd round the cattle-stall said a young woman had thrown a bucket of water over the squire, but he had been on the edge of the crowd and not seen anything of that.

Several times he returned to the hiring section in case she was looking for employment. The one place he knew she would not be was the wife-selling arena.

He went home at the end of the day feeling exhausted. Of course she might not have gone to the fair, knowing he would be there, but he had to try and it was the best place if she hoped to find work. What now? He resolved to visit again, every day the fair was there, which would be almost a week, he knew, in case she assumed that he would only go once and so would not be hiding from him on subsequent days.

In bed that night he tried to think where she might go for refuge. Not to her family. Her mother was dead and she couldn't abide most of her relatives. Not to his family either. Nevertheless he knew he must question them all just in case.

Three days running he went to the fair. He searched and he talked to people who might have seen her; after all she was striking enough for people to remember, but there was no sign of his beloved wife. After those three days he had no heart, nor could he really spare the time, to attend again. He had done his business there on the first day and common sense told him it was foolish to waste energy on the unlikely chance of seeing her.

He rode over to his mother's farm one morning. They were surprised to see him and he couldn't tell them why he had come. When Joseph asked about Betsy he said she was busy at home, that he had to come this way and thought he would call in to see how his mother was. He knew it sounded plausible.

He also knew that Joseph was disappointed

because Betsy wasn't there. He told himself again that there was nothing in it, that Betsy was beautiful and she could not help the attraction she had for men. It had nothing to do with her feelings – she did not encourage it yet it still happened. He truly believed this – and yet she had left. She had denied an alliance with Thomas Shooter and although he desperately wanted to believe her it had looked bad.

Now, suddenly, he knew her denials had been true: there had been nothing between them. Thomas Shooter had made it up and tricked them both. He was sure of it. That boy who brought the message was the key. Betsy had tried to find him and prove her innocence. Daniel felt dreadful. He knew now, without a shadow of doubt, that she was innocent, that he had to find her and bring her home. He cursed his wretched temper that had made him threaten something he would never carry out, to threaten her with the very thing she hated so much, one of the practices they were both trying to stop. He must have been mad. His head drooped on to his chest as physical pain attacked his body. He must rest, he could not afford to be ill. Jim was a good lad but he, Daniel, was needed here on the farm.

For the first time since Betsy had left Daniel slept the night through. Maybe it was sheer exhaustion, he thought, but whatever it was, when he woke he felt more refreshed and ready to tackle his work than he had done for days.

At the end of the week he decided to take a trip to Betsy's family. They had not seen them since the day of her mother's funeral and he doubted any of them would know where his wife was, but he needed to try everything and everywhere.

As usual he did all that was necessary on the farm, leaving Jim working and in charge, and he took the trap over to Betsy's home village. He didn't hold out much hope, but there might be something there that would give him an idea of where to look next. He did not expect to find her there, but if he could have a clue then he would follow it to the ends of the earth. Life without Betsy was nothing and if she would only come back to him he would ask nothing more for as long as he lived.

Richard arrived at the Salden cottage first. He saw the same man who had eventually answered the door on his last visit. He was just as unkempt but a little more forthcoming. Probably still expected money, Richard thought and decided to play along with this. 'I'm still looking for Betsy,' he said. 'It's important to find her soon.'

'Why?' The man's eyes were bright with curiosity and what Richard was sure was greed. Shaking his head he said, 'I can only tell Betsy.' As he turned away he added, 'Are you a close relative?'

The greed was definitely showing in the man's watery eyes at this. 'Her uncle. Her mother's brother and looked after her like she was my own when she was little.'

Richard suppressed a smile at this blatant lie but he moved forward as if to go inside the cottage. 'Well, in that case perhaps we should talk. Shall we go in?'

Although he had spent much of his life in the shadow of his elder brother, Richard had his own kind of charm and determination. If this relative could lead him to Betsy, who he was sure was in some kind of trouble, then he was prepared to compromise his natural truthfulness.

He was surprised to find that the room they entered was clean and there were two comfortable-looking armchairs each side of the fireplace. Although the family obviously neglected the outside of the place, the inside was looked after. He sat in the chair the man indicated.

'You must be wondering about my interest in finding Betsy,' he said quietly, 'and I will tell you why, but first I need to know your name so I do not give our secrets to the wrong person.'

The man's eyes bulged with excitement. Richard, who was prepared to say he was a relative of Sir Richard Choicely in order to get Betsy's uncle to talk, had no need of the subterfuge.

'I'm Betsy's Uncle Jack. Her mum died last year y'know. She were my sister. Hard life she had and she always did her best. I helped her a lot – I've no childer of me own and Betsy were like a daughter to me.'

It seemed that once started the man couldn't stop. The prospect which he obviously had in mind, of his niece coming into money was making him reckless.

'There were a bit of scandal years ago,' he looked directly at Richard, 'but me sister, she didn't hold any grudges, even though she got nothing from Betsy's father. It were a struggle to bring her up, with the other kids y'know, but she never beefed, though the man what did her wrong was rich. I can't tell you his name because I promised her mum I never would.'

He looked down to his boots and once again Richard tried to hide a smile. He stood up. 'I must be going,' he said. 'If you see Betsy would you tell her Lord Lampney was enquiring after her. I am not Lord Lampney,' he added quickly as Jack Salden's eyes glinted at him, 'but I am close to him.' He moved to the door and opened it at the precise moment that Daniel Forrester's clenched fist was raised to knock on it. Instead of hitting the door the blow connected with Richard's chin.

Richard reeled backwards, almost into Jack's Salden's arms. 'Hells bells!' he said.

On recognizing each other the two men immediately guessed why each was here. For Daniel was the thought that Betsy had gone to Richard Choicely – why hadn't he thought of that, and the thought occurred to Richard that Betsy truly was missing, or Daniel would not be here and looking so worried.

'I'm sorry,' Daniel said. 'Are you all right?'

Richard touched his nose carefully. 'Yes I think so. Bit of a shock though, but it was an accident. No hard feelings.' He held out his hand.

Jack Salden watched this with a sulky expression on his face. 'Your precious wife's not here,' he said to Daniel. 'Left you, has she? Gone off with someone?'

'Not at all,' Daniel said. 'I came to see her Aunt Agnes.'

'She's not here. Don't know when she's coming back.'

Richard joined Daniel outside.

'Just a minute,' he said. 'Where is she?'

'She don't live 'ere.' Jack closed the door.

'Would she be likely to be with her aunt?' Richard asked Daniel.

'Who – my wife? Of course not. It was Aunt Agnes I was looking for but you heard him say he didn't know when she would be there.'

They had reached the trap standing in the lane now and Richard said quietly, 'I saw your wife not long ago when I was visiting in Graceden village.'

Daniel looked up sharply, 'You did?'

'Yes.'

'She does go into Graceden sometimes.'

'It is worrying when someone is missing,' Richard Choicely said quietly. He studied the other man's face.

Daniel looked up sharply. 'What makes you think she is missing Sir Richard?' He hated asking but obviously Richard Choicely had some knowledge or he would not be visiting this cottage now. Had Betsy gone to Chasebury Manor and tried to find her father? He realized that the other man was speaking. 'Sorry, what did you say?'

'I said perhaps we should combine our efforts to find Betsy. Something is obviously wrong.' Daniel was silent. After a moment or so Richard said, 'When I saw her she was looking for a boy who lives in the village.'

'I know. She found him. He – he caused some trouble at the farm and now Betsy has left.'

'I also saw her at the fair a few days since.' Richard volunteered the information tentatively.

'You did? I was there several days and never saw her.' There was no pretence on Daniel's side now. All he wanted was to find his beloved wife. He no longer cared that Sir Richard, or anybody else, knew she had disappeared. If telling them would help lead to her that was all he wanted. Richard felt for the farmer. If Betsy was missing and no one knew where she was no wonder he was worried.

A slight movement from the window of the cottage made them move away. Jack was obviously watching and wondering.

'How did you travel?' Daniel said.

'By carriage, but I left it with my coachman a mile or so outside the village and walked in.'

'I can take you back there,' Daniel said.

'Thank you, that would be welcome.' Richard climbed on to the trap, Daniel flicked the reins and they set off. As they turned the corner leading out of the village they saw a woman walking in.

'That's Betsy's Aunt Agnes,' Daniel said. He drew on the reins and handed them to Richard, then hurried over to her.

'Hello,' he said. 'It's Aunt Agnes, isn't it? I was wondering if you've seen Betsy this last week?'

'I have not and I hope I never see her again. Mislaid her, have you?' She strode away down the lane.

Chapter 10

Sir Richard Choicely and Daniel Forrester might seem to be unlikely companions. Yet circumstances had drawn them together. Daniel was ready to take advice from anyone who might have knowledge of his wife's whereabouts, and Richard claimed to have seen her at the fair.

Richard Choicely wanted to find out whether she was his brother's child and he also wished to follow up the thought expressed by his father's late gamekeeper, namely that his brother Benjamin's accident was in fact not an accident at all, but murder.

On top of all this he was tremendously attracted to the beautiful Mrs Betsy Forrester. For now however he and the farmer had one common purpose: finding out what had happened to Betsy. They pooled their knowledge of the last time she was seen by each of them.

'Betsy does not get on well with her family,' Daniel said, 'so it was really a forlorn hope that she had contacted them. There are several aunts and uncles and she dislikes them all. They were cruel to her when she was a child,' he said quickly by way of explanation. He did not say that her Aunt Agnes had told her she had a different father from the rest of the family, and that his name was Choicely.

Richard, in his turn, did not mention the likeness to the maternal side of his family, nor why he too was concerned for Betsy. They parted amicably but with a promise to let each other know when any news of Betsy came.

Back home Daniel did wonder why Sir Richard was so interested in Betsy when he had only seen her a couple of times at most. Was this another case of Betsy's power over men? Or had she approached him on the possibility of her being his daughter? No, she would have told him. In any case Richard Choicely himself would surely have hinted at the possibility this afternoon if he had any idea about it.

He went out to the fields. There was a lot of work to do and these last few days he had put most of it on to Jim. For the time being he must get out there and look after his farm for everyone's sake.

When Betsy ran from Richard Choicely at the fair she instinctively made for Rosa's caravan. To her great relief both Rosa and Bill were there. 'We are talking about moving on tomorrow, Betsy. Have you thought what you are going to do? Because you are welcome to come with us, you know.'

'I should like that,' Betsy replied.

'There are a great many fairs at the moment and we shall stop for a while at the next one. If we leave in the early hours of the morning we shall arrive before it has got going and we shall have the pick of the work.'

'I must pay you – I have the money I earned this week before they threw me out.'

'No. You may need it later and there is plenty of room here. You pay in friendship Betsy, not in money, yes?'

Rosa's words made sense and Betsy hugged her. 'I will always remember your kindness,' she said quietly, 'and maybe one day I will be able to repay you.'

'There are other ways than money. To give women a voice because someone gave you a chance, never give up on that.'

Betsy had told Rosa and Bill about how she had learned to read and write when she was with Mrs Wallasey at Wren Court and a little of the devastation she had felt when that lady died. She shuddered and Rosa put her arms comfortingly around her.

They bought their sausages and eggs from old Will's stall the night before they left.

'We're moving out tomorrow, Will,' Rosa said. 'Take care of yourself now.'

'I will, gal. You too, mind. An' that pretty wench you've befriended. Ah, not much misses my old eyes, Rosa,' he added, noting her surprised expression.

'Will's an old pal,' she told Betsy, who was waiting on the edge of the throng jostling to buy his food. 'We look out for each other. You ever get to a fair without us, go see him. He'd never let you starve.'

They set off on their journey at three o'clock the next morning and had the road to themselves.

'Later,' Bill said, 'the lanes will be blocked with carts and animals and people all travelling to the fair and we shall be there cooking our eggs and sausages, and ready to start work again.'

The road was rough and rutted, in some places more than in others, and under the trees it was just a muddy track. Bill and Rosa knew every inch of the way and the horse clopped steadily on through the moonlit night. Twice they had to cross a ford and once a narrow bridge and Betsy found she was enjoying this quiet, unusual journey. She and Rosa talked some of the time and were silent at others, in a warm companionable silence which brought a modicum of peace into her heart. That and the calmness of the night, only punctuated by the calls and movement of wildlife gave her the hope that she would find steady work to go to when the fair was over.

They were amongst the first to arrive,

having stopped in a clearing a mile or two from the site and partaken of a hearty breakfast and fed and watered Patch, their horse.

The three of them soon found work in different areas of the field. Betsy was kept busy all morning and only once, when she was washing down a cow which looked so remarkably like Sadie, did she find her eyes filling with tears as she remembered the night they had tried to save her.

Blinking them away she said softly to this one, 'They say you all look alike, but you don't, you know.' The animal gazed back at her, its velvety brown eyes sad.

She was so tired by the end of the day she fell asleep almost as soon as she climbed into her bed. The caravan was comfortable and during the next few days Betsy thanked God each night for her friends and her surroundings.

'If it hadn't been for you two I might have been wandering from place to place with no money to buy food and no shelter and safety,' she said.

'You would have found something, Betsy, but we are glad to have you with us until you and your Daniel are back together again.'

Betsy turned from the little stove where she was on cooking duty. 'That's not going to happen. It was no ordinary quarrel we had, Rosa.' She took a deep breath and said, as steadily as she could manage, 'There is something I haven't told you. Daniel bought me in the market three years ago.'

There, it was out. It was the first time she had told anyone how she came to be Daniel's wife, the first time she had said aloud those dreaded words.

'He bought me as he would a cow or sheep,' she added, her voice catching on a sob.

Rosa walked over and laid an arm round her shoulders. 'But you fell in love with each other later. I can see you did. That is the important part, not the way it began. Women will change all that given time, but love will go on for ever. You love Daniel, and although I have not met him, from all you've told me he loves you.'

'So much that he would not throw away the straw halter he led me from the market place with.' Turning into Rosa's arms she sobbed bitterly.

'I'm sorry,' she said as her crying subsided, 'I ran because he was going to sell me again.' Shivering now at the memory of seeing him through the window, holding the straw halter, she lifted her head high and said with as strong a voice as she could muster, 'He thought I was unfaithful. I wasn't. Someone tricked me and Daniel believed him.'

Reaching up she touched her locket, hidden beneath her dress now in case a thief in the markets tried to steal it if it showed.

Rosa had seen it earlier and said softly, 'Daniel gave you the locket, didn't he?'

Betsy nodded, 'I would starve rather than part with it.'

'We won't let you starve,' Rosa said in an attempt to lighten her friend's thoughts, 'and we can protect you from other men, although from what I've seen you do it well enough yourself. Come on, we'd better get this meal ready, don't you think?'

Sir Richard Choicely consciously tried to think about the girl he was to marry in a few months time. He had known Lily Aston Jenkins for two years now, and he liked her very much. Was fond of her even, but he knew he didn't love her. Not as he had loved his first wife. When she died a great chasm opened in his life.

Lily was an only child and moved in the same circles as he did. The family originally came from Devon and moved to the Kent/Sussex borders two and a half years previously.

Richard's eldest son would one day inherit the title and the manor and he realized that with this new marriage he could have other children. He and Lily had talked about finances and were in agreement over all of it.

'I am twenty years older than you but everyone will be provided for in my will,' he had told her not so long ago. 'My two sons and any children we may have together. I also have an eye for a property a mile away which I shall buy. It is not large but large enough and it will be in your name so you will have independence when I die.'

'Richard,' she said, half-laughing and half-crying, 'We are about to get wed and you talk about dying.'

'We need to sort things in a proper manner,' he replied gently. 'I am sure there would be no problems but this makes everything legal.'

He thought about his forthcoming marriage now and for the first time since his proposal wondered if he was doing the right thing. The feelings that Daniel Forrester's wife stirred in him were worrying.

It wasn't simply the physical stirrings thing, he could get those anywhere, it was a protective feeling too. Did this stem from the fact that she could possibly be family? He had found himself fantasizing about her more and more lately.

Now he was in touch with her husband, even, to an extent, helping him to trace her, and his mind was in turmoil about Lily. He did not want to cheat her. He knew many cases where men married to carry on the name and estate, but he had no need of that. He already had two sons.

Yet life would be easier for him if he had a

wife. Someone to grace his dinner-table, someone to turn to and trust. He and Lily liked the same things. She was a placid girl, or she seemed so, and when he pushed her on the age question she told him she liked older men. He had no desire to be a father-figure to her, but he knew now that she did not excite him as the girl who was Daniel's wife, and possibly his niece, did.

He and his brother Ben had always been so different in their looks and ways. He knew the situation wouldn't have worried his brother when he was alive. He would have married the suitable one and taken the other whenever he fancied. But that was not Richard's way. Betsy had inherited the maternal line physically, had she also inherited it mentally? Had she in fact run off with a man? Was she as wayward as Ben? Now he was presuming she *was* his brother's daughter and he knew he must be on his guard against this. The girl might be nothing to do with the Choicelys at all.

'I need to know,' he muttered to himself, 'and if she is Ben's child I must find out whether her mother killed Ben.'

He rode over to Daniel's farm early one evening, realizing that the man would be busy outside during the day. He tried to think of a logical reason for calling on the farmer, but abandoned the idea quickly. It would surely be seen through and he disliked pretence anyway.

Daniel had just sat down to his evening meal when Richard arrived. His reaction on seeing the man there was alarm. 'Sir Richard,' he said. 'What brings you here?'

'I was in the area and wondered if you had news of your wife yet? I ask because I visited the village earlier and discovered from my henchman who lives there that the boy she was looking for is called Zac. Of course you may already know this.'

'I didn't know his name.' They were both silent for a moment, then Daniel said, 'It doesn't matter now anyway. As you know she has left.'

'Yes and I am sorry. If there is anything I can do to help find her just say. You have a farm to run while I have more time for searching.'

He left the question in the air and Daniel said, 'But why should you, Sir Richard? It is a kind thing to offer, but for what reason?'

'You were good enough to look after one of my men some time ago,' Richard said quickly, 'and one kindness deserves another. I travel further afield perhaps than you do, and your wife is very beautiful. If she is in a certain area it is possible that someone will know.'

Daniel offered Richard some ale and as he raised his own glass to his lips he said, 'I would come to wherever she is should you discover her, Sir Richard.'

'I realize that. I will keep my eyes and ears open. You have no idea where she would run to, I suppose?'

'If I had I would have been there,' Daniel said quietly. 'There is nothing I can tell you that would help. You have seen her home and family and I have asked questions of my family. It was most unlikely she would have gone to either of them, and she hasn't.' Suddenly he put his head in his hands, 'I pray to God she is safe,' he said in a voice thick with emotion. 'She is strong-willed and could put herself into great danger.'

The two men shook hands when Richard left. As the sound of the horses' hoofs disappeared Daniel wondered again why Sir Richard Choicely was so interested in Betsy. Had he any idea of the possible link between her and his family? Was he indeed her father?

Chapter 11

Betsy, Rosa and Bill left the day before the fair finished. 'Will give us a good chance to be first at the next one,' Bill said, laughing. Betsy, who thought she would have to say goodbye to her friends when they all moved on, was to travel with them as far as the next place. 'After that I must go my own way,' she said. 'it isn't right to burden you like this.'

'You are no burden,' Rosa said, 'and you may find work at the next place. We will be travelling in a sort of arc so you will not actually be going much further away than you were before. You don't want to be too far away from your home ground, after all.'

Betsy looked at her warily. 'Why, Rosa?'

'Because Daniel will find you more easily. From what you tell us he can't leave the farm for long enough to travel great distances, so it makes sense to stay as close as possible.'

'But we are not together any more.'

'Not now you aren't, but you will be. Come and help me with this bag, will you, Betsy?' When everything was packed and ready Bill saw to Patch, the horse, and Rosa went outside and looked around. Betsy joined her to gaze at the throng over in the main part of the field.

'Rosa, do you truly believe Daniel will come looking for me?'

'Yes, I do. I feel it in my bones.'

'But he was going to sell me. He said so.' She whispered the last three words. 'That's why I left.'

'Have you never said something in anger and regretted it, Betsy?'

The girl nodded miserably. 'I couldn't

stay, though. He was looking at the halter and I was never going to have that happen to me again. Never, never, *never*.'

Tears welled in her eyes and Rosa put an arm round her shoulder, 'I can't *see* what will happen. My grandmother could, but I haven't inherited her gift. But I do *feel* things that come true and the vibrations for you and your Daniel are strong. I'm telling you the truth as I feel it Betsy. Come on, Bill's ready.'

They arrived at the fair just outside Canterbury later that day and when the horse was fed and watered the three of them walked into the city. They bought food and drink and went into the cathedral.

It was the first time Betsy had been there and she was enthralled. Before they left she knelt down and prayed that Rosa was right and that Daniel would look for and find her. Then she added another prayer that he would stay well and always prosper whatever happened. The anger at what he was going to do was far, far below the love she felt for him. Even if she never saw him again she could wish him no harm.

Back at the caravan they made a meal and then sat outside in the balmy evening air until the sky darkened. A few others began arriving on the field before they went inside, and when they looked early the next morning the field was half-full of stalls and people. The fair was coming alive.

This was a three-day fair and Betsy found work on the second day. She decided she would go for a live-in position and so joined half a dozen others in the line for kitchen work. She did not mind standing there and being looked over for this purpose. She needed work and this was the best way of finding it. The man who hired her and the girl standing next to her worked for Lord Aston-Jenkins of Clover Court.

'Wonder what this place will be like,' the girl said. 'I'm Marie and my last place was awful. The son of the house had his hands all over the place – I couldn't wait to get out.'

'I'm Betsy.'

'Where did you work before this?'

Betsy had already decided on her story. She would say her first job had been her last and hope that any would-be employer would not question it.

She turned to face the girl. 'With Mrs Wallasey at Wren Court. She died,' she added, 'so that's why I'm here.' Neither the girl and, which was more important, her future employers questioned it and she breathed freely again.

She hoped she wouldn't have to share a room with Marie, who seemed a nice enough person but Betsy didn't want to have to talk about her personal life to strangers. It

199

might be difficult not to do so with the chatty and friendly young woman being taken on with her. She needed to fit in and not be thought of as high and mighty, as she had once heard herself described.

Clover Court was a lovely country house and Betsy was relieved to be given a tiny room almost in the eaves. But it was hers and private. She and Marie were given the choice of one of them sharing the lower room with the two others already in residence or using this very small attic. Betsy quickly said she would be happy with the attic, which seemed to suit the garrulous Marie.

It was strange at first being entirely alone again. Since the age of ten, when she had shared with the two girls at Wren Court, there had always been somebody there. George, her first husband, then Daniel, and recently she had been sharing with Rosa and Bill; now suddenly she had a small space which was hers alone.

She worked in the kitchen with Marie. The cook was a large, jolly lady who said to them both on that first strange day, 'There are two rules in my kitchen: No taking food out and no lads hanging round the door. Obey them and we shall get on well.'

Betsy was happy enough with those. The other two girls who were already employed worked mostly in the house, although they came to the kitchen for their meals. These were eaten with the cook and butler at each end of the scrubbed table and were companionable occasions.

She was lonely however, especially for the first week because, from what Marie said, the three of them who were sharing a room chattered and laughed and Betsy was isolated from this. Not that she wished it any other way, but lying in the narrow iron bed at night she couldn't stop her thoughts from returning to the bedroom she had shared with Daniel. She missed Dumbo too and wondered whether the cat looked for her and was sad. Such silly thoughts, she chided herself as she turned into the pillow to stifle her sobs.

A month later Richard Choicely came to dinner. He had been before but because he was referred to in the kitchen as Miss Lily's fiancé Betsy hadn't known who he was. One of the upstairs maids, who also waited at table, had been poorly all that day and by the evening had to take to her bed. Marie was chosen to take her place because she had experience of waiting at table.

Remembering the harvest suppers, the kitchen at home, and Mrs Wallasey's beautiful dining-room Betsy smiled to herself. She had not volunteered more information about herself than was needed to be a kitchen-maid and was content for matters to remain that way, at least for the time being. Possibly not for ever she thought, as she watched Marie parading round the kitchen with a silly grin on her face.

The meal looked and smelt delicious and later, when Marie was sitting at her place next to Betsy and eating her own meal she said, 'Miss Lily's fiancé is so handsome, isn't he?' She gave an exaggerated sigh, 'I think I like older men really, she *is* a lucky girl.'

'Yes, well, that will do,' cook said quickly. As they washed up together, Marie whispered to Betsy, 'I expect I shall dream about Sir Richard Choicely tonight. He smiled at me you know.'

Betsy just saved the plate she had in her hand, and let it slide back into the soapy water. 'Is – is that his name, Marie?'

'Mmm. So good-looking in a manly way, not like some of the silly boys who make passes. Mind he's *ever* such a lot older than her. Funny, isn't it, 'cos you'd expect her to marry someone her own age, wouldn't you? But I s'pose there aren't any suitable ones, don't you?'

Fortunately Marie was so carried away with her exciting evening she didn't seem to notice that Betsy was not really answering, just murmuring her agreements.

As soon as everything was finished and away and the kitchen floor washed ready for the following day she said goodnight and

202

went to her room. Sitting on the edge of the bed she let the facts roam round her mind.

Richard Choicely, the man who *could* be her father, was going to marry a girl who was only about her own age. Why not? she thought, after all, Daniel is much older than me, even George Hatton was older, but Richard was different. She thought of him as Richard and not Sir Richard now, and more and more she thought of him as the father she never knew.

Although it had been such a shock at the time she discovered it, she believed her Aunt Agnes had spoken the truth. The knowledge made her uneasy, especially if it had been as Aunt Agnes said. Yet having met the man she could not imagine that it was. She preferred her own version of what she thought might have happened. The two sisters enticing him and her mother being the one he chose.

After all he was a man and that said it all. Perhaps he never knew about the baby – she pulled herself up sharply – it was more likely that he did know and his family paid her mother off.

He would have only been a young man at the time and he obviously married later because Daniel said he was a widower with two sons. Strange to think that if it were all true, those sons were her half-brothers. Betsy no longer knew if she wanted it to be true or not. She only knew that she must never venture from the kitchen area because if Richard saw her he might tell Daniel. Of course they would only meet at the market or the fair and in the normal way of things they would not know each other. But because of the encounter with Sir Richard's groom the acquaintance had been made and Betsy knew that he would not pass her by without speaking, nor pass Daniel without enquiring about her.

She shivered as she recalled her last meeting with him at the fair when he told her he had seen Daniel and that he was looking for her. She needed to be very careful or the situation could so easily get out of hand, and much as she longed to be with Daniel again, the risk of being found was far too high.

Chapter 12

Daniel had never felt so low. For a week he haunted the fair, sure in his mind that Betsy would be there. Often he could not spend too long looking because of the work on the farm, and when he returned he would get himself something to eat and then work until the light beat him. Jim had been marvellous, working extra hours and keeping things going in every area. Daniel had also taken on another girl from the village to work in the dairy with Hannah, the young dairymaid they already employed.

Sometimes he looked at the straw halter, still hanging on the hook and wished he had never made such an issue of it. Betsy had hated it yet it was the only material thing he knew that would keep her with him. Rubbing a hand across his weary eyes he suddenly admitted to himself that it would make no difference. She would stay because she loved him as he loved her.

Where was she now? Where would she go? Then, in a sudden flash, it came to him. Back to Wren Court, the place where she had been happy when Mrs Wallasey was alive. If she found a job there again she would have a bed and food. There was only one way to find out and that was to go and see. Sick with apprehension he knew he could do no more that night. He must find out exactly where the house was and in a few days' time, when things were straighter here, he would pay them a visit.

For the second time in weeks, Daniel slept through the night and woke feeling better. Of course, she might not have done that, but at last he had made a decision that might have results. He refused to think about her not wanting to come home. He was sure she had gone on the spur of the moment and it was all because he had mentioned the fair, but Betsy knew what a temper he had, she must surely know he had not meant it when he said that awful thing about taking her there. He could not even remember exactly what he had said, he had been in such a state, but the image of her shocked face was with him still.

It was the weekend before Daniel could get over to Wren Court. He thought it would be better to go to the tradesmen's entrance rather than the front door. He took with him some butter and cheese and set off with great hopes. Betsy had told him about the house often and about her special lady. He knew that her son now owned the property, the son whose wife had arranged Betsy's first marriage to George Hatton. Betsy had glossed over the reasons but Daniel thought he knew them anyway.

He was jealous that he had not been the first with her but all he wanted now was to have her back with him. He missed everything about her. The kitchen seemed unwelcoming and he seldom had time to go into the sitting room. His bed was desolate without her, many times he reached across during the night simply to touch her, feel her, know she was there, and when his hand felt the empty space he was devastated as he remembered how it had been. He went to bed each night with the nightdress she had worn the night before she left. It still smelt of Betsy and offered a tiny crumb of comfort to his aching heart.

The woman who came to the kitchen door knew nothing of Betsy. He told her he was looking for a relative who had at one time worked there, and she said the place had recently been sold. 'We have been here only a few weeks. None of the old staff is left,' she said, 'I think some of them went with them.' She did not know where the Wallaseys had gone, 'but I think it was somewhere abroad.'

Not that that mattered he thought as he returned home, because it would have been Wren Court that might have attracted her, not the Wallaseys themselves.

He tried to look at the situation dispassionately. She would need to find work and the most likely place would be in one of the bigger houses or farms. Somewhere she could live in. She must have been at the fair the week she left because it was the obvious place and if she had found work on the first day he had probably wasted all that time looking in the wrong area. People came from miles around to the fair and Betsy could be anywhere by now.

Lily and Richard were to be married in the spring. Plans for the wedding were discussed during dinner one evening. After the meal, partaken in the oak panelled dining-room, the family had coffee in the garden. There were three lawns, a great many interesting shrubs and trees and a magnificent rose-bed, which in the summer was ablaze with colour and a joy to the nostrils, so sweet was the scent of the flowers there.

The orchard was at the far end of the garden, but this evening the family held their tête-a-tête on the small lawn in front of the drawing-room windows.

'The marquee will be set up on the big lawn,' Lady Aston-Jenkins said. The discussion went on for some time, then the chill in the air drove the family back indoors and cook sent Betsy to collect the cups from the garden. Usually the upstairs maids did this, but only one was on duty. the other having been sent off earlier in the evening because she wasn't well.

'Go and get the crockery from the tables on the small lawn Betsy,' cook said, 'then we can clear up. They won't be wanting anything else tonight.'

Knowing that Richard had been to dinner again Betsy hoped cook was right in her surmise that the family were safely indoors. She went quickly, pausing beneath a tree for a quick survey of the area. There was no one about. She dashed over to the white table and chairs set out on the lawn. Quickly she piled the cups and saucers on to her tray and hurried back in the direction of the kitchen. To do so she had to cross in front of one of the windows of the house and Richard was standing there. He had his back to the window and she scurried by, praying that he would not turn round and see her. Head down, she turned the corner that would take her along the path towards the kitchen. There was no cover here and she was almost running as she reached the back step, missed it and went sprawling, the tray and fine china clattering to the ground.

Betsy's ankle sustained a sprain that necessitated her doing all jobs in the kitchen sitting down. She managed the stairs to her room that night with help and from the attic to the kitchen the morning after her accident by bumping down each stair on her bottom. Returning in the evening, she was aided by Marie, who reported that her room-mates were both in love with Sir Richard Choicely.

'Meself though, I can't see what the fuss is about. He's only ord'nary, and too old for the likes of Miss Lily.'

'You've changed your mind,' Betsy said spiritedly. 'Last time he came you were over the moon about him.'

'Well, I've 'ad time to think, and he'll be an old, old man when she's still young and pretty. I wouldn't want that. I reckon as she'll look around when she's wed and find herself someone younger.' Marie winked.

'You know, unofficial like.'

Betsy was indignant. 'Why should she? She'll have a good life with him. He's a charming man. And he doesn't *look* old.'

'No, not yet, I'll give you that, but old against her. I mean his hair's grey for a start, well, more silver really, quite nice – here, how d'you know what he looks like? You haven't ever seen him.'

Betsy thought quickly. '*You* said so, didn't you, Marie? Last time he came, you told me how young-looking and handsome he was.'

Her smile was radiant as she looked at the other girl, but her heart seemed to be going at double its normal rate. She had given herself away now. But Marie frowned and said, 'Did I? I don't remember. Anyhow, he's not for the likes of us. More likely finish in the market-place, eh? But somehow I've never fancied that meself. I mean, having men look you over like. I'd rather be chosen proper, know what I mean? It's different when you're just looking for work. That's all right.'

Betsy, not trusting herself to speak as she realized she had got away with it, said, 'Yes, I know what you mean. I feel like that too.'

'With your looks you'd never have to, though,' was Marie's parting shot. 'Can you manage now or d'you want me to get you anything?'

'No, I'll be fine, and thanks Marie. See

you tomorrow.'

Whew, that was close, she thought. She must be careful.

Although Betsy's bad ankle inconvenienced her she was extra helpful in the kitchen, doing whatever she could sitting on a stool, and hobbling around when necessary. Marie, who, unlike the girls who had been with her at Wren Court, was not jealous of her beauty, fetched and carried and chattered. Her one taste of working upstairs had been a highlight and she talked about it constantly. What the room was like, what they talked about, 'mostly the wedding,' and of course, 'Miss Lily's intended.' That she had only been up there on that one occasion made no difference. Listening to her you would imagine she knew them all well, Betsy thought, and she was more on her guard than ever when Sir Richard Choicely's name was mentioned.

At night, in her narrow and rather hard bed, it was Daniel and not Richard who occupied her thoughts. During the day she was busy and tried to concentrate on her work, but alone in her tiny room at night she did not try to stop thoughts of him crowding her mind. She pictured him on the farm, with the horses, with the cows, and getting himself a meal when work was over. Closing her eyes she saw their bedroom and felt his arms round her, his caresses and kisses the most real thing of her days and nights now.

Was he missing her? Or had he shrugged the whole thing off? I shall never go back unless he seeks me, she thought one night as she brushed away the tears that had seeped from her closed eyes. That he could have even contemplated 'selling' her was the most hurtful thing ever to have happened to her.

Remembering Rosa's words she thought that *if* he said it in temper, and she admitted to herself this possibility now, then he would try to find her. But how? No one at her mother's house would know and that was the only place he could try.

She had no idea when she had come to this household as kitchen-maid that it was the home of Sir Richard Choicely's fiancée. If she had realized that she would not have taken the position.

Her panic at finding Richard upstairs and then trying to conceal herself from him began to take on a new aspect. If she could be sure, as her friend Rosa seemed to be, that it was all a dreadful misunderstanding, then she would return to Daniel. But how could she be sure? And would he want her back.

They loved each other, but they were both stubborn people and, miserable as she was without him, she would not risk the straw halter. After their three years together she knew that his beliefs had not changed, and if he had not been going to hold it over her at some time then he would have taken it down long ago. It was the one thing he had been utterly firm about on the few occasions when it had been mentioned.

Determinedly she lifted her head. *Maybe I am in a better position than I expected to be,* she thought. *At all costs I must hold on to this position.* She slept better that night than for some while, in spite of the ache in her injured ankle.

Chapter 13

Sir Richard Choicely's elder son Benjamin, who was at public school, was visiting for a few days and Lily and her parents came over to Chasebury Manor for a meal one evening. Benjamin had been named for his uncle because all the Choicely boys were named Richard, Benjamin or David, which was confusing when more than one generation was present. In this instance of course there was only one Benjamin and one Richard there.

It was a pleasant evening and after dinner they had coffee on the terrace. Benjamin had met Lily before but not her parents, and it was quite a jolly family party who watched night descend over the garden. The moon shone on the shrubs and trees which stretched into the distance, making them glow both romantically and eerily.

'This is such a beautiful place,' Lily said quietly to Richard, 'it's exactly right, big enough to entertain yet not too large to be homely.'

'You will be happy here, won't you, Lily?'

'Of course. If I am with you I will be happy wherever we are, Richard.'

He took her hand in his and squeezed it gently. 'What a lucky man I am,' he said softly in her ear, then, turning to the others, 'Shall we go inside, the air becomes more chilly about now.'

When they had left in their carriage after Lily lingered for a last goodnight kiss, Richard went indoors, but did not go straight to bed. Instead he went into his study and took from the desk the drawing he had done of Betsy Forrester. Why did that woman's face haunt him? Was it those eyes that he knew he had not quite captured in his sketch? Eyes that had depths and colour such as he had seldom seen. His mother and brother Benjamin had both been blessed with expressive eyes, but Betsy's made you catch your breath. He wondered what it would be like to hold her in his arms and lose himself in the sea of changing shades of blue. What it would be like to let his hands stroke her long black hair, to kiss those lips, to undress her and... Angrily he thrust the drawing from him and strode round the room, his body on fire.

After a restless night Richard decided to try and see Betsy's aunt, the one they met on their way out from the village the other week. Aunt Agnes, Daniel had said her name was. She had refused to talk to Daniel that day but it was possible she hadn't noticed another man in the trap. Not enough to recognize him from that distance, anyway. If he judged that family correctly she would see him if she thought there were money or titles involved. It was certainly worth a try.

The following day he took his son back to school, then he thought about how he would tackle Betsy Forrester's Aunt Agnes.

There were two items on his agenda. The first was to endeavour to trace Betsy's whereabouts, although he suspected from what Daniel had told him of the background there that Agnes genuinely did not know, because neither Betsy nor he had had anything to do with her family after her mother's death. Yet Aunt Agnes might come up with a name or connection if he could persuade her to talk to him.

Number two was to sound her out about the events of twenty-one years and more ago. He decided he would be Lord Lamp-

215

ney, the name he had used when he spoke to Betsy's Uncle Jack. If his enquiries over the past few months had been on the right lines then Agnes Salden, or whatever her name was now, should be able to reassure him. Not that he expected her to do so, not if it *had been* her sister who tied the rope between the trees to kill Ben. But if he saw her and spoke to her himself it would give him the opportunity to see whether it was a realistic possibility.

He had no doubts that the old gamekeeper Pike had been telling the truth when he told his son about the rope and the woman he had seen later. Richard drew two trees on the pad in front of him and stretched a rope between them. He made another drawing of a hooded woman taking the rope down and lastly he drew a final picture of the back of her disappearing through the trees. The rope was probably coiled up and held beneath her cloak.

If only Pike had mentioned the incident at the time. Yet what good would it have done, he thought? Young Ben had had liaisons all over the county. There were many women who might have sought revenge. It might not have been Betsy's mother after all. Nevertheless he wanted to pursue the thought. There was not much chance of proving anything after all this time, and in any case the woman herself was dead now, but his tidy mind wanted to sort the matter out for his own satisfaction. It would establish for him whether Betsy was a blood-relation of the Choicelys.

Two things happened to prevent Richard carrying out his plan immediately. Lily's mother was taken ill and a week later her father was out with the shoot and had an accident with a gun. It was not too serious, resulting in a nasty but not life-threatening wound to his leg. He too was confined for a while and Lily was fully occupied in running the household.

Richard rode over to Clover Court most days or evenings and once he thought he caught a glimpse of long glossy black hair and a shapely Betsy-like figure. Then he told himself he must be dreaming, that the girl was haunting him and he was seeing what wasn't there.

The woman he saw had been coming from the stables and he was too far in the distance to see more than a general outline. It had been such a fleeting sighting. She had turned the opposite way to the drive and then dis-appeared, so she was obviously not staying in the house. From where he was he could not be sure how she was dressed, but her clothes were dark and her hair gleamed in the half-light of the early evening. He had already stabled his horse and been walking over to the house. He stood for a moment in case she reappeared, then he chided himself for his fancifulness. Probably one of the servants been sent over to the stables for something.

As Lord and Lady Aston-Jenkins recovered Richard's visits stopped being daily, although he still went several times a week. Lady Aston-Jenkins looked fragile but the doctor was pleased with her progress. She was able to leave her bed for several hours now and Lord Aston-Jenkins sat with her most afternoons. 'It is quite sweet really,' Lily said to Richard one day. 'I believe it frightened Daddy tremendously when he thought he might lose her. For all his blustering ways he relies on Mummy's judgement in so many things.'

Richard had grown fond of them both. His relationship with his own parents had been overshadowed by his brother's preferential treatment, although he had not discussed this with Lily.

His own feelings for his brother had been of admiration as well as envy. Looking back he supposed there had been a little jealousy but in truth not a great deal. Ben was the eldest, the heir to the estate and as such he had certain privileges. Richard accepted these as right.

What he *had* yearned for had been the magnetism his brother possessed. He could see from this distance in time that Ben had charm but not integrity. When they were both young he had longed to be blessed with even just a little of this attractiveness, but for many years now he had realized how shallow his brother was. Richard was happy with himself now that he was older and he owed a great part of this feeling to Anne, his first wife and mother of his sons. When she died he was devastated.

His feelings for the farmer's wife were something he must keep to himself. They were the normal urges a man feels for a woman, he told himself, nothing more, nothing less. Just thinking about her gave him an erection. The fact that she could also be his niece made him feel guilty and he remembered Ben saying to him one day years ago, 'The trouble with you, Richard, is that you are too pure to have fun – well, that will never be said about me. Take what you can while you can is my way.'

We were total opposites, Richard thought, and while I longed to be like him, deep inside me I knew, even then, that I could not. You cannot go against your nature and be happy. And he had been happy until he lost Anne.

When he thought about Lily, the young lady he was going to marry in the spring he knew that he *did* love her. Differently from the manner of his love for his first wife, but he wanted to share the rest of his life with her and it was a good feeling. His desire now was to make her happy. He recognized that part in himself that wanted to be needed, and felt that he was indeed a fortunate man because Lily was young, pretty and she loved him. He hoped and believed they would be happy together.

Or is this all sentimental nonsense? he thought. It is I who needs someone permanent in my social life, someone to grace my table at dinner parties, someone to have in my bed at night, someone to relate to as a friend as well as a lover. Lily has the same beliefs and background as I do and our marriage will be good. I shall make sure it is. After all the Choicely coat of arms was, *Duty first, all else shall follow.*

Betsy was torn between keeping out of Richard Choicely's way and making herself known to him. During the normal running of the household she need never see him because she was based in the kitchen, but if she wanted to she could slip out and be waiting somewhere. She knew he would stop the carriage if he saw her; he seemed the perfect gentleman. A man she would be proud to have for a father.

While acknowledging at last that the story Aunt Agnes told her *might* not have been the truth she still thought that it was. She had never really belonged in that family, never been part of the fabric as her brothers and sister were. As a small girl she remembered being bewildered when she tried to please and had been cussed for it. She had recognized the resentment among them all against her, but her childish mind didn't know or understand what it was. She only realized that everyone else was together and she was an outsider. Now, knowing that she had a different father from the rest of them did not seem surprising.

Aunt Agnes said he was the son of Sir Benjamin Choicely of Eccleton. Sir Richard Choicely was the son of Sir Benjamin Choicely of Eccleton. There could be no mistake. She could not afford to be wrong. Before she confronted him as his daughter, though, she had to be sure, doubly sure. And she would not go to him for shelter in any case because she knew she could make her own way. That she wanted the acknowledgement of her birth did not detract from the independence which was vital to her and which she had been fighting for most of her life.

Daniel had fought with her. He believed in this as she did, and although she had done nothing to further her cause since living here, it had not gone away. The fact that there was nothing to complain about here was not the issue, she thought. There were many households which were not as good as the Aston-Jenkins home and estate.

Her yearning for Daniel grew worse rather than better but no man would ever own her again. No man would ever buy or sell her in the market-place or anywhere else. She was Betsy Forrester, a woman who had a brain and a heart and who could read and write and was equal to anyone, man or woman.

She loved Daniel, loved him beyond anything she could ever have envisaged for herself, but even he would never have the opportunity to threaten her with the straw halter a second time. She would live her life feeling half-alive without him as she did now, rather than risk that again.

Betsy began to plan her career. Certainly she did not intend to stay a kitchen-maid for the rest of her life. She could work her way through until she was a housekeeper or cook. She would be in charge of some part of a house, even as she had been at her beloved Redwood Farm with Daniel.

Always when these thoughts threatened to engulf her she remembered her special lady, Mrs Wallasey, and sat quietly for a while to think what she would advise. She knew how fortunate she had been when she was a child of ten to have met and worked for a true lady. One who, although her own status was assured, had seen and helped those who were not in that position.

'Not everyone will, or even can, aspire to

do great things,' she used to say, 'but if you believe you can, then you will, Betsy. Learn all you can, watch and listen and work out how you see things in your own mind, no matter what others tell you.'

Although it was so long ago when Mrs Wallasey died and Betsy's world fell apart for the first time, some of the tears she shed now were for her special lady as well as for her beloved Daniel.

Chapter 14

Richard decided to approach Betsy's Aunt Agnes through her brother Jack. He thought it unlikely that he would be able to find Betsy through that source, but there was a chance that she knew the name of Betsy's father. If her sister had confided in her, and if she now thought there was a possibility of money, she might talk to him about that. He did not much like the method he was going to use, but having exhausted all else, he wanted the matter settled in his mind.

Strange that now all the participants in that drama were dead, he found himself pursuing the bits that had not tied up. Of course he had been too young at the time and with too little comprehension of the events, although the snatches of remembered conversation among the staff in the kitchen had stayed indelibly in his mind, he had not consciously thought about them for years.

His parents had presumably never known about the rope. Which left only a handful of people with the knowledge. Jim Pike, the gamekeeper's son, one or two of the maids who might have heard the rumour but were long since gone from Chasebury the old cook, the butler and himself.

He had no idea where the kitchen-maids were now. The cook was dead and the butler ga-ga. Richard visited him sometimes, at least twice a year, at Christmas and Easter, taking him a basket of seasonal goodies. He lived with his daughter who was married to a farmer in a village a few miles away. His mind had been going for years and he had not recognized Richard at all for the last two visits.

No, the best way was to find the sister and try to discover whether she knew anything. At least he might learn whether Betsy *was* his brother's child, but he doubted she would tell him if her sister had murdered his brother because of it, even if she knew.

Yet there was the possibility that her sister might have confessed before she died. People often did. Old Pike had told his son what he had seen, after all, long after it was too late to do anything, but it was a link. If he could find other links it would help. Richard realized that the mystery had taken charge of him.

After his wedding plans, which were number one at the moment, but were more in the Aston-Jenkins's hands than in his, finding out whether Betsy Forrester was family was the next important task.

Then came the gruesome subject of murder. Richard was convinced now that his brother had been killed. That the rope stretched between the trees had not been there for someone to practise jumps but had been deliberately set up to murder his brother. He felt sick at the thought. They had not been close and he had deplored many of Ben's ways, but murder by any means had to be addressed.

It occurred to him that it might not have been Betsy's mother alone, that brother Jack or indeed any of the family could have helped. But that would mean too many people in the know. And tying a rope across, hiding amongst the trees so she could take it down as soon as the accident happened, then going off through the woods herself was something that needed no accomplice.

Richard surmised that she had told no one at the time. She had, after all, gone on to have the baby. Had she passed it off as her husband's child, he wondered? He frowned: there had been no mention of her husband yet it seemed the most likely idea. The thought that she might have confessed, possibly on her deathbed, would not leave him. Her sister Agnes was the one whom Richard thought would be the person she told the full story to, if indeed she had told anyone. It was Agnes whom Daniel Forester was trying to see that day when he had met him in Marshdean, he recalled.

Several things began to take shape in his mind as he remembered the Beaumonts, his mother's side of the family. Betsy had the Beaumont features, the Beaumont charm, the Beaumont colouring, all the things he had once longed for. How did she fit in with that dreadful Salden family? It could explain why she had gone into service when she was ten years old, though none of the others appeared to have done so. He was extremely thoughtful as he set out on his journey.

Jack Salden invited him in rather grudgingly. 'What d'you want now?' he said.

'A chat with your sister Agnes.'

'She's not here.'

'Where could I find her? It is very important,' Richard said.

'You can tell *me* what it is.'

'I'm sorry, but I cannot. This information has to be given to Agnes and no one else. So you see she will never know what it is if I cannot speak to her.' Richard's voice kept an even note as he said the words and he even smiled slightly because Jack looked so pleased. It was obvious that the man smelt money.

'Well, in that case no harm for you to know. She lives in Ivy Cot, other end of village.'

Richard thanked him and set off to track down Agnes. She was not pleased to see him and only his foot in the door stopped it being slammed in his face.

'If you will not talk to me,' he said, his voice quiet but firm, 'then I shall have to look elsewhere for my brother's child. Which would be a great pity.'

She looked sharply at him, then said quickly, 'Why? Why would it be a pity?'

'I cannot discuss family business out here. May I come in for a moment?' His words had the desired effect and she opened the door wider to let him enter the room.

'Well, what family business, Sir Richard?'

She did not ask him to sit down and he stood towering over her. 'Your sister's baby,' he said.

'My sister had several children,' she said.

'I think you know that I am talking about Betsy.' His voice was quiet.

'What about her?'

'I believe she had a different father from the others.'

She jerked her head up aggressively. 'What's it got to do with you?'

Keeping his naturally low, deep voice gentle he looked at Agnes's angry florid face and said, 'I'm not sure at the moment, but I am trying to find out. If my family is involved I want to know because nothing can be put right if I do not have the knowledge of what happened twenty years ago.'

'You *know* Betsy's Ben's child,' she said. 'Have you at long last decided to admit it and give our family what your father should have done years ago?'

'I know nothing except what you can tell me, Agnes. I do not even know the name of Betsy's mother, but I–'

'Name of her mother, name of her mother – Ben didn't bother with names, all he wanted was a woman and every woman had what he was after. It didn't matter to him whether it was her or me, or – or anyone. A washerwoman was as good as a princess for his purpose. Your brother was a scoundrel and he deserved all he got.'

'What do you mean by that?'

'Well, he died before his time, didn't he? Got his come-uppance. The Almighty struck him down and made him pay for his sins. It didn't help my sister – *your* family left her to struggle on–'

'If what you say is true,' Richard rested his hand on the table near where he was standing, 'maybe my family knew nothing of it. Have you thought about that?'

'Of course your family knew about it. My sister went to see them and was insulted and worse. Your high and mighty mother sent her packing. Her son had his fun and my family had to suffer for it. If you've come to offer money now I'll take it and give it to Betsy. It's some sort of justice at last.'

Richard shook his head. 'I have come to find Betsy,' he said. 'Any business I have must be done with her, not through a third person.'

Agnes moved quickly considering her bulk, and Richard found himself being pushed roughly towards the door. 'Coming here under false pretences, making me think you were going to do the decent thing. You're no better than him. Scum, that's what he was. But mine until that night, and his daughter's like him, arrogant hussy.'

She had opened the door with her other hand and as her meaning hit him he said, 'Yours? Is Betsy your child or your sister's? Answer me. It is important.'

His foot was wedged against the door again and now he used his strength to prevent his being ousted. 'Well?' His hands were on her shoulders. 'You've had your say, now I want the truth.'

His usually quiet eyes were blazing and she quivered slightly under his gaze before shouting, 'She's hers, of course. She was always jealous because it was me he came for and she had her revenge that night when he was so drunk he didn't know who he had.'

Her lips tightened into a thin, ugly line and her face contorted with rage. 'She didn't get rich and she hated the child, but he never lived to do it again, did he?' Suddenly she lifted her head and spat in his face.

Richard returned to Chasebury Manor, his mind seething with the revelations. Betsy was undoubtedly family, she *was* his brother's child and what Agnes said was consistent with what he already knew or surmised. What he had not known was that Ben had been involved with both sisters. He tried to remember the exact words which burst from Agnes's angry lips.

'Scum, that's what he was but mine until that night.' She had also said something about his drunken state and it was all of a piece with how his brother had been. Drink and women.

Obviously Betsy had no idea of any of this and for a few moments he contemplated leaving things as they were. Then he knew he could not. This was something he had to do. Apart from any other consideration he had already committed himself by talking to Agnes about it.

Betsy Forrester was his brother's child and

she was in trouble. She had run away from her husband for whatever reason, and at present he could not conjecture why, but he had seen her in the market and she had run when she saw him. That reaction had become easier to understand once he knew that she had left Daniel Forrester. But still both he and Daniel had no idea where she was, and a woman roaming the countryside alone was in danger. Especially one as beautiful as Betsy.

Maybe he should talk to the farmer and tell him about the connection with the Choicely family – yet what use would that be? No, the answer was to find her and take it from there. The bitterness of the Salden family was understandable as far as wanting money for Ben's child went, but nothing warranted killing Ben. Nothing.

When Betsy's mother had been unsuccessful in her attempts to obtain money or recognition – and he could imagine his mother's scathing remarks and denials on behalf of her elder son – then she should have stopped short of murder.

That night Richard dreamt he saw Ben racing through the woods as he used to do, much too fast, being thrown as the horse reared or even touched the rope, then backed away. He saw a woman in black, with her back to the figure on the ground, lurking behind a tree several yards away.

Suddenly she turned and looked at that deathly still form; then, swirling her cloak more closely around her she made off in the opposite direction.

Richard gasped, then woke up, sweating profusely. The face he had clearly seen in those few seconds was a younger version of the woman he had been talking to this very afternoon: Agnes Salden.

Richard rose and walked over to the window. The full moon was bathing the garden below with a ghostly whitish-yellow light and he shivered. Agnes had killed his brother. Not Betsy's mother, but the woman his brother had apparently spurned. He thought his brother's murderer was dead but she wasn't, she was alive and even now trying to obtain money from his family.

He moved from the window and paced the room. Of course it was only a dream, but it was vivid. And it made sense. It was Betsy's mother who had come to see his parents and gone back empty-handed and un-acknowledged. It was Betsy's aunt, the one Ben had been dallying with first, who had wreaked a terrible revenge after he scorned her for her sister. God, what a mess. And yet out of all this came Betsy, the woman he had not been able to get out of his mind since he first set eyes on her. The woman he too was secretly hankering after.

Agnes sank into a chair and rested her heaving shoulders on the table. She remembered how it used to be when Benjamin Choicely came for her at least twice a week. Oh she knew she wasn't the only one, but she was young and vibrant and she knew how to please a man in bed or, as happened most times for her, under the trees in the woods. Sometimes, especially in winter when the winds blew and the rain pelted down, Ben would take her on the back of his horse to a hut hidden in the forest just beyond the Chasebury estate. There on a bed of straw they made passionate love to each other.

Benjamin Choicely had been the man of her dreams, and although she knew he would never marry her she was happy to let things go as they would. He was the sort who would always need someone else and she intended always to be that someone. Her stupid sister was prettier but she was dull, deadly dull, when it came to men. Look at the one she had eventually married and had umpteen children with? And look at the child she had the one time Ben took her?

She raised her head from the table now, and began to wonder. Was it only the once? She had always presumed so, but...

'He was mine,' she said to the empty room. 'Oh, he had strumpets all over the county, but he always came to me twice a week. That stupid cow of a sister had to be the one to get with child, and never me. He wouldn't have cast *me* off like that. I would have stood up to his mother and father and anyone else, they'd have had to have set me up properly and looked after me if they wanted to marry him off to someone more suitable.'

She banged her fist on the table until it hurt. 'And this is Richard, the younger brother who is now the heir. And what of Betsy? The inheritance ought to be hers. She is Ben's child, but she's a girl. If only she had been a boy I would have helped in the fight all those years ago because Betsy would have inherited, and we'd all have benefited, but all she got was her father's beauty and her father's nature. I've always hated her. I still hate her.'

After a while she rose and poured herself some ale. She could feel her heart thumping and knew she needed to calm herself. That stupid girl had always got on her nerves. As a baby she had been far more appealing than her own children. As a child she had a certain haughtiness not apparent in any of her cousins, and every time she looked at her Agnes saw Ben. How she had kept it to herself all those years was hard to believe now.

Ben had deserved to die and she had planned his death because he never returned to her and after all the glory months no one else satisfied her. But the last straw was her sister. That sealed his fate. That he went to her and she was having his child was too much. She tried three times to see him; she knew that he was avoiding their entire family because of the expected birth. 'Stupid cow, she should have got rid of it or made him provide. I would have.'

She recalled how she used to wake in the middle of the night, remembering how it had been and realizing that it never would be the same again. She had not minded the others, but to spurn her for her own sister was more than flesh and blood could stand. That was when she knew he had to die.

She knew his ways so well and was confident she could carry it out. If she was never again to enjoy the ecstasy that was Benjamin Choicely then neither should anyone else, especially that sister of hers who was pregnant with his child.

Now, after all these years, his brother had the nerve to come here and say he would only do business with Betsy – Betsy who was the reason she lost Ben. Betsy – the child she had hated since her birth. Agnes nearly choked on the weak ale she was drinking, and, spluttering with rage as each thought chased around inside her head, she paced the small room. That was another thing: how did he know where she lived? And where *was*

Betsy? It seemed everyone was looking for her and no one knew where she was? First had come that disagreeable husband of hers, Daniel, and now Richard Choicely too.

If she found Betsy before that high and mighty Richard Choicely she'd tell her a thing or two, by God she would. But where to start looking for her niece? She seemed to have disappeared completely. Probably with a man somewhere, Agnes thought. Like father, like daughter. Well, if that girl was going to come into money she, Agnes, was going to have some of it for herself and her family. But especially for herself. That would be some sort of justice.

Chapter 15

After returning from a delivery of milk to Graceden, the village three miles away, Daniel stopped by the church, tied the horse to the railings and went inside. He slipped into a pew at the back, knelt down and prayed that Betsy was all right, that she would send word to him. If only she would do that he knew they could sort it out. He loved her and he was as sure as he could be that she loved him, but the straw halter was more like an iron band between them. The remedy was in his hands, he knew, but if he never found her again what could he do? If he did find her – and he would never give up looking – then his first act would be to get rid of it. As it was he tormented himself with looking at it every day as a form of punishment.

When he came outside a few minutes later he wondered about the boy Betsy had said lived in this village, the one who had come with the message that someone was in the stable. But it didn't matter to him any more. He simply wanted Betsy to come home. Finding the boy was not important. He had himself driven away the person he loved. It had not been easy at first to understand that she loved him too. Throughout his life he had never known such happiness. He had always been the ugly and unwanted one. His youthful liaisons with women had been loveless, and until he brought Betsy to Redwood Farm he had little real passion or tenderness in his life. He unhooked his horse and cart and turned for home.

He was busy on the farm and Jim was tact itself, never mentioning Betsy in Daniel's hearing. One day Daniel said to him, 'Meals aren't as good now the mistress isn't here, Jim, but I do my best.'

Jim looked solemn and a bit embarrassed and Daniel said, 'It's all right, lad. We'll manage but there won't be any apple-pies until she comes home.'

He saw Jim's surprise and added, 'She'll be back one day.' Silently his mind and heart said, *please God,* and then the two men were quiet as they ate their bread and cheese.

He was down the bottom field when Jim came to fetch him. 'Some people to see you, master. Said they were called Rosa and Bill.'

'Rosa and Bill?' Daniel racked his brains but he could not think who they were. He knew nobody called either Rosa or Bill, he was sure.

'I'll be down in a few moments. Will you keep your eyes on them, Jim?' He finished his job and walked down to the farmhouse. The couple were outside talking to each other.

'Mr Forrester, I hope we aren't intruding, but we met Betsy several months ago and as we were in the area we just called in to say hallo.'

'I'm so sorry. She isn't here just now. She won't be back today,' Daniel said rather too quickly.

'Oh, what a shame.' Rosa looked disappointed, 'We have to move on and don't know when we shall be this way again. Never mind, we mustn't keep you, I expect you are busy.' She held out her hand. 'Nice to meet you. Perhaps we may look in next time we are this way again?'

Bill proffered his hand too and Daniel, frantically trying to find words that would give him news without letting them know Betsy was missing, said, 'I ought to offer you refreshment and if my wife were here she would do so, but she's away nursing a relative just now and we are short of workers.' The lie came suddenly and easily.

'That's fine,' Rosa said, her deep voice soft with concern for him. 'We just came in on impulse.'

'I'm glad you did. Where – where did you say you met my wife?'

'At the fair in – where was it, near Canterbury a couple of months ago, wasn't it, Bill? We go to so many of the fairs and meet so many people that it's sometimes difficult to remember which one was which.'

'Yes, of course it is. We – we *were* at the fair, Betsy and me, on – on several of the days,' he said.

Rosa began to walk away and Daniel said, 'I'll tell her you came by. She'll be sorry to have missed you, I know.'

He watched until they were out of sight. Damnation. Why hadn't he found out more. They knew of him, knew his name and that Betsy lived here, or had done. How had Betsy met them, in what way were they her friends? Wearily he turned back towards the fields.

The fair near Canterbury, he thought. That wasn't the one he had been to. But Betsy had told them where she lived. Hope soared in his heart. She would not have done that if she hadn't wanted them to seek her out. Did it mean she meant to return soon? His step was lighter as he went back to the bottom field, and Jim, watching him from the cowshed, noticed this and hoped those two people had brought good news to the master.

Rosa and Bill walked the two miles to where they had left the caravan in a field belonging to a farmer acquaintance they often met around the fairs and markets.

'That poor man, he's under a dreadful strain,' Rosa said, 'but I'm glad we've seen him now and who knows, we may be able to get them back together?'

'Now, Rosa darlin', leave well alone,' admonished Bill. 'We mustn't interfere. You've done what you wanted and met Daniel, now leave things be. It's not our concern.'

Her eyes were smiling as she turned to him. 'Yes it is our concern, Bill, because Betsy's our friend. She's desperately unhappy without him and that man we've just left wondering who we are and how we are involved in her life, is pining for her too. I could feel his pain.' She laid her hand over her chest.

'I love you, my Rosa, but you're a fussy old mamma sometimes. Betsy became like a daughter to you, didn't she?'

'Yes, I suppose she did, and we are in a wonderful position to bring them together because we know where they both are. Don't fret, Bill, I shan't do anything until the time is right. And maybe we won't need to do anything anyway, the good Lord possibly has his own plan.'

Bifi slipped his arm round her. 'I'm sure He has, so He doesn't need help from you.'

'No, but they do. Betsy and Daniel. A little nudge in the right direction. She knows where he is but he doesn't know where she is, *yet.*'

'Rosa.' There was an affectionate warning note in his voice.

She turned into his arms and kissed him long and tenderly. 'I love you, Bill. Come on, we're nearly there, I can see the caravan.'

They moved on a few miles that evening, and later, cosily in bed after their loving, with Bill snoring by her side, Rosa thought again about Betsy and Daniel. She had indeed grown very fond of the young girl and maybe Bill was right about the daughter bit. They had not been able to have children and she accepted this as part of her lot in life, but it never stopped her from dreaming.

This particular dream had not occurred for some while, but it was vibrant now and she decided they must soon turn the caravan towards Lord and Lady Aston-Jenkins's home and see how Betsy had fared.

Rosa slept well and it wasn't until the following morning, when she went outside to watch the sun come up over the fields, that the awful fear that Betsy might have moved on from Clover Court came to her.

Betsy decided she must find another place before the spring and Lily Aston-Jenkins's wedding. It was possible that she and Marie would be asked to help upstairs at some stage of the proceedings. It was a small staff and although so far she had avoided doing this she feared it would come.

Under normal circumstances she would have relished the idea, but not now. Richard Choicely would recognize her, she pulled a rueful face, there was something to be said for being nondescript, one of a crowd. She had always stood out, as a child and as an adult, and it had seldom brought her anything but trouble.

Once Richard Choicely was part of this family the dangers of their meeting would be greater. Yet there was one part of her that wanted him to see her and possibly tell Daniel where she was. Although why would he do that? Of course he would not. He had no interest in her beyond the politeness that, she realized, he extended to everyone he met. She and Daniel had helped one of his men and he would not snub her, wherever they met. Yet when she saw him at the fair he had said that Daniel was looking for her, which might mean that he would send word to Daniel.

Since working here she had heard what a good man he was. Cook had been introduced to him and one day, in one of her more talkative moods when they were having their meal, she had told them how he said he spent a lot of time in the kitchen of his home when he was a boy.

'He said it gave him a taste for kitchens which were usually warm and happy places. Miss Lily will be well-suited with that one, for all that he is older and has been wed before.'

'I reckon as to how cook's in love with Sir Richard,' Marie said to Betsy one morning when they were alone in the kitchen peeling the potatoes. Betsy laughed and tried to change the subject but Marie would not be moved.

'He is a lovely man,' she said. 'Not for the likes of you and me of course, but he looks so romantic and he has such a wonderful smile. When I was upstairs,' she said *'upstairs'* with a kind of swagger, 'and I served him, he looked right at me when he said thank you.'

Cook returned then and even Marie knew better than to indulge in discussion of the family when she was around. Betsy privately thought it was Marie and not cook who was in love with Richard Choicely and smiled to herself when she thought that she might, *just might*, be his daughter.

Cook herself opened the back door when Rosa called. 'I was in the area, my caravan is along the lane at the back,' said Rosa, 'and I wondered if I could have a word with Betsy, who's the daughter of a dear friend of mine.'

Cook looked across the room, 'She's busy right now. Betsy, do you know this woman?'

'Yes, cook.'

'Well, if you want to chat you can go at five for one hour. That's if you have everything prepared for dinner this evening. You must be back by six – do you understand?'

'Yes, cook. I will be,' Betsy said quietly. They usually were finished by five anyway and had an hour where they were allowed to go to their rooms if there was nothing urgent to do in the kitchen, so cook wasn't really giving her anything. Still, it would be best to keep on the right side of cook, who wasn't a bad sort really, Betsy thought.

She sent a dazzling smile across the room to Rosa, who, with a quick 'see you soon then,' to her and a warm, 'thank you so much,' to cook, quickly left.

Betsy fairly flew round the kitchen doing everything in double-quick time and being as helpful as possible. At five minutes before the hour everything was spick and span and ready for their return at six. Cook looked round and said, 'Off you go, Betsy. Back by six, remember.'

Betsy ran up the narrow stairs to her little attic room, took off her apron and brushed her hair, then hurried down again and across the courtyard. She felt incredibly excited. It would be wonderful to see Rosa and Bill again.

She was half-way down the lane when she saw Richard Choicely on his horse, coming towards her. He was still a good distance away, so she dived into the hedge until he had gone past.

Meanwhile Rosa had set out to meet her. She saw her figure in the distance, and as she raised her hand to wave, Betsy suddenly disappeared. The man on horseback said 'good evening' as he went by but Rosa was far too worried about where Betsy had gone to do more than smile at him. She *had* been there, she was sure of it, and she hadn't been anywhere near the horserider, yet she had vanished. She began to run along the lane now, and her relief was mingled with amazement as a dishevelled Betsy emerged from the hedge.

'Goodness, you gave me a fright.'

'Sorry Rosa, but that was Sir Richard Choicely riding by and I didn't want him to see me.'

They hugged each other and, taking her arm, Rosa said, 'Why ever not? You weren't doing anything wrong, and it's not like you to avoid possible trouble. Or has this man been making a nuisance of himself with you?'

Betsy laughed aloud, 'No Rosa, not in that way, but there is a reason I didn't want to see him. I'll tell you about it soon, but not now; let us enjoy this hour together. Tell me where you've been and what you've been doing and how Bill is?'

Within a few minutes they were cosily inside the caravan, which was resting a few yards along the lane with the horse tethered to a nearby tree. Bill hugged her too. 'It's good to see you, Betsy. We've cake and a drink, Rosa's special, the one she makes from the berries and herbs.' The hour sped by and at twenty minutes to six Rosa said, 'We will walk back with you, Betsy.'

'There's no need, it isn't far and I shall be all right.'

'We want to, don't we, Bill?' Without waiting for an answer she went on. 'You might meet the mysterious horseman again.'

Betsy said, 'He is Lily Aston-Jenkins's fiancé and a very nice man.'

'That's why you took a header into the hedge,' Rosa said, laughing. 'It's all right, Betsy, I won't be nosy, but we shall go all the way with you in case there is any trouble about.'

They left her by the back entrance of

Clover Court. With a last wave Betsy ran in and up to her room to get her apron and at two minutes to six she was in the kitchen ready for work again.

In bed that night she thought about her position in this household. If she stayed she was very likely, either before, during or after the wedding, to meet Sir Richard Choicely. Earlier this evening she had decided she must move on, now she reassessed the situation and there did not seem to be the same need. They would meet as family and maid if they met at all, and once Miss Lily was married even that possibility was less because he wouldn't come over here as often. If he enquired about her or tried to talk to her it would simply be because he had met her in other circumstances.

She saw that she was being foolish over this because looked at sensibly it was most unlikely that he would concern himself one way or another. Pursuing the idea that he could be her father must wait until later when she could check the facts. For now she needed to concentrate on working as well as she could here.

She dreamed of Redwood Farm that night and of Jim and Daniel coming in for their meal, of Dumbo rubbing round her legs and sitting on her lap in the evenings, and of Daniel putting his arms round her and telling her he loved her.

When she woke the next morning she burst into tears. The dream had been so real. Slowly she brought her mind back to the present and went across to the tiny window to look down on rooftops and chimneys and far, far below, the courtyard where she had stumbled as she ran so that Sir Richard Choicely would not see her.

Chapter 16

Agnes thought a great deal about the past after Richard Choicely's visit. Betsy was obviously missing and would have to be found. It seemed that the Choicelys and her husband Daniel had no idea where she was, but both were searching.

'Reckon as to how young Richard Choicely stands the best chance of finding her,' she mused to herself. 'The farmer hasn't the time or the means.'

She thought of the owner of Chasebury Manor as young Richard because that was what he had been when she was involved with his family all those years ago. She had made plans then and she would make plans again now. Not murder of course, there was no need; Richard was not like his brother physically or in any other way, but he had as good as admitted to her that he knew Benjamin was Betsy's father.

Her heart was pounding now and she felt more alive than she had for a long while. She would make the family pay for Ben's wicked betrayal twenty years ago.

She had known then that there was no chance that he would marry her but she had loved him passionately and longed for his child. She would have been all right because she would have fought for hush money. His child would have been beautiful and clever and he would have set them up and visited sometimes. She would not have been jealous of whomever they made him marry because he would still have come to her and the wonderful hours of their lovemaking would have been all she needed.

But it never happened. In all the months, almost a year, when she regularly met him deep in the woods, when she listened for the sound of his horse and that first glimpse of her hero and lover, she never got pregnant.

When she knew her sister was carrying his seed she wanted to kill her. Instead she murdered her former lover and later married a man from the village who died four years later, leaving her with two sickly and dull children. Comparing them to the bubbly and beautiful Betsy she transferred her venom from the mother to the child.

Now if, after all this time the Choicely

family were prepared to admit the truth she would take what was her due. Betsy, that little upstart shouldn't have a penny for herself.

But she had to do it through Betsy and Betsy was missing. She gave little thought as to why, or even what had brought this searching for her about; it was sufficient that they were all trying to find her. Unless her niece had told Daniel, the only people still alive who knew the full story were herself, Betsy and, it would seem, Sir Richard Choicely. Well he wouldn't push *her* around as his brother had pushed her sister.

She drew her lips tightly together. The first thing to do was to find her missing niece. When she did she would have to work out a way of threatening her so that she, Agnes, could have a share of the money.

At the forefront of her plans was the fact that she could be rich if she went about things in the right way. A cottage and an amount of money each week for the rest of my life, she thought. That's not much to ask for what I went through. The only difficulty will be in getting these things from the Choicelys when they have got away with it for so long. Richard might give Betsy money but she knew neither of them would look after her.

Agnes let the matter bide for a while. She said nothing to her brother who, she realized now, must have told Richard where she lived. As it turned out this was all to the good. Jack Salden was as greedy as his sister but, no matter what his suspicions were, he had never known for sure and he had been too young at the time to work out what was going on.

The idea came to Agnes as she lay in bed that night, going over in her mind Richard's visit and what he had actually said as he was going through the door. It was when her temper flared and she had felt again the jealousy of twenty years before.

'He was mine until that night,' she recalled shouting, and then his reply as he misunderstood her words. 'Is Betsy yours or your sister's?'

She felt her blood rising so that it nearly choked her. 'Got you,' she said aloud. 'Benjamin Choicely, though you are dead and gone you will pay me for what I went through.'

Jubilantly she sat up in bed and waved her arms around. She had to convince Richard that Betsy was really *her* child and already a scheme was forming in her head. She could tell him her sister had pretended the child was hers to protect Agnes, who was walking out with a local lad. She would say that her sister, already married and with a large family, could have passed the child off as her husband's, even though he was seldom home.

As she was now the only one alive who knew the real truth, she could bully Betsy into supporting her with money if the girl believed that her aunt was her mother. Agnes had always enjoyed a challenge and this one would go some way towards giving her what she thought of as her proper due.

Richard Choicely wouldn't know that none of her family would have lifted a finger to help another, any more than that brother of his would. Oh yes, clever Sir Richard had set the thing in motion himself with his remark, she thought.

She tried to recall the rest of that conversation but it wasn't easy. She had got angry and had shouted the truth: that of course Betsy was her sister's child, but she could always say she was in a flurry and repeating the story that was put around at the time. Now there was no longer any need to protect her sister's memory, nor her own reputation, and she could tell the truth, that the child was really hers. Yes, that's what she would say. That part would be fairly easy, the difficult bit would be tracing Betsy. Because if they couldn't find her there would be no money.

By the following morning Agnes knew what she was going to do. Go to the woods, those same woods just outside Chasebury where she and Ben had made love so often, and watch for Richard. If he took the carriage he would obviously leave from the front entrance but if he rode, which she was sure he often did, then she would track him. It would take time and patience but she had plenty of both now.

During the next few days she found out he had a fiancée named Lily Aston-Jenkins. That made things really easy because she only needed to find where she lived and how often he visited. Some of his other trips would have to be looking for Betsy and she would shadow him on those whenever she could.

She was hampered inasmuch as she had no transport to call on, but she had her legs and they had not let her down yet. Chuckling to herself she thought that Richard would do the work in finding her niece and she would step in at the last moment and claim Betsy as her own child.

For the first week there was nothing except sore feet and tiredness but the following one saw her in the lane near the Aston-Jenkins's place.

Richard had ridden over earlier one afternoon and today she had walked but halved the journey by cutting across fields. She sat on the verge with some bread-and-dripping brought from home and waited to see what would happen next. It was very quiet apart from insect sounds and after a while she decided it was time to explore.

Because Richard was there and could recognize her she stayed away from the front of the house and went to the servants' entrance. She wasn't sure what she was going to do; probably mostly kill time waiting for him to return and try to see where he went next.

The more she thought about it the more she felt certain that he was the one who could lead her to Betsy. She believed he had no idea where Betsy was now, but he seemed determined to find out. She had spoken to her brother Jack and discovered this wasn't the first time Richard Choicely had been to their village. 'Pretending he was a friend of Lord something or other,' he had told her, 'but he was from Chasebury right enough. He was one of them – 'e didn't fool me.'

Better not be too much in the open. She hurried along a narrow path and, spying a couple of bushes shielding the side door from part of the garden she decided to take refuge behind them. From here she could watch without being seen for no one was likely to wander round near the servants' quarters except the servants themselves.

A happy thought struck her as she realized this could be another source of knowledge about Richard Choicely's movements, for staff usually knew far more about the comings and goings of the big house than they should.

There was another thing: Betsy had been in service before she married the farmer so perhaps she had gone back to that life now. Someone from these quarters might know where she was; it could be worth while to try and talk to one of the servants.

By now Agnes was feeling happier than she had for years as she foresaw her dream of revenge and money coming closer. From being a sour might-have-been it was rapidly becoming a sweet possibility.

She was taking a huge bite from her bread-and-dripping when she heard footsteps. Cautiously looking round from her hiding place she could scarcely believe her eyes when she saw her niece hurrying along and letting herself into the servants' quarters.

When Agnes saw Betsy entering the servants' domain of Clover Court she could have shouted for joy. Did Richard Choicely know that his niece was working for his fiancée's parents? Hardly likely, she reasoned, or he would not have been looking for her. At last things were going right for her.

She stayed behind the bush for a few moments longer to stem the excited trembling of her body. She had found Betsy and she knew that so far the others looking for her had no idea where she was. How best to turn this to her own advantage? If she told either of the others she would lose control of the situation. If she told Richard only she still wouldn't be in a good position.

She needed to put her plans into action quickly now. First she had to convince Richard Choicely that Betsy was *her* daughter and not her sister's child. And she had to do it before she revealed where the girl was working and before Richard found out for himself where she was.

Another thought came into her head. Had Betsy deliberately found herself work here to have access to Richard if she wanted it? The possibilities were endless but so far she, Agnes, had all the cards. Fate truly had played into her hands today. Moving cautiously so as not to be seen from any windows she walked quickly along the path that led to the back lane.

She had only gone a few yards when she realized that her bag containing her purse and the remains of the bread-and-dripping were by the bush where she had been hiding. She turned and went back, not seeing the man who emerged from a private path a few yards further along.

Richard Choicely, for it was he, saw her and after a few seconds spent waiting to see if she reappeared, hastily went after her. He kept to the side of the hedge a good distance behind and she never looked back. Once into the open area she kept her head down and made for a bush not too far from the kitchen door. She wasn't running but for a fairly bulky woman she was going pretty fast, he thought. She reappeared, clutching a canvas bag, just as he reached the end of the lane. She stood there for a moment and as he covered the distance between them she said, 'Why, it's Sir Richard Choicely, isn't it?'

'It is. What have you got in the bag?'

'My purse and I had some bread-and-dripping in there, but I've eaten that now.'

'What are you doing here?'

She had her answer ready, 'I was out walking and saw this lane and wondered where it led. I put my bag down while I looked around because I saw I was in a private garden, then thought I had better not stay. When I got out into the lane again I remembered my bag so I came back for it.'

'Do you know whose house it is?'

'No,' she lied, 'whose house is it?'

'It doesn't matter. Only that you should not be here. You are trespassing.'

'I know that now but I didn't at first. I've done nothing wrong,' she said. 'I told you, I came back for my bag.'

He knew there was nothing he could effectively do or say. She wasn't stealing although she might have been looking around with a view to doing just that. He had no proof.

'Just don't come here again,' he said, his normally gentle voice harsh. 'These people are friends of mine and if I find you have been here, for whatever reason, you will be in trouble.'

As she turned to go he added, 'Don't doubt that. I shall make it my business to enquire and there will be big trouble if you are found here again.'

'I am not a thief,' she retorted, 'if I had come to steal I would not be having a picnic in the grounds.' She took a couple of steps, then looked at him.

'Go on,' he said, 'you've had fair warning. As it happens I don't think you came to steal. I don't think you wandered in here by accident either. Maybe you had come to look and check the place out for someone else, but I shall be watching everything very closely from now on, so don't try any tricks.'

She moved towards the alleyway into the back lane and he followed her closely. At the bottom she turned to him and said, 'You think you're so high and mighty, don't you? You could be in for a shock soon when you learn the real truth about Betsy's birth, *Sir Richard*. You were too young to understand what was going on at the time, but I shall tell you the truth soon.' She set off quite quickly along the back lane.

Richard decided against returning to the house and reporting the incident. It would be difficult because Agnes would be sure to let them know she knew him and that he had in fact called on her.

He wondered what she was doing there. Who was she looking for? Him possibly, maybe to see if finding him would lead her to Betsy. She was a cunning woman and, he was sure, a murderess also, but as yet he had no proof. At that moment he hated his elder brother. He was no closer to finding Ben's daughter Betsy and at a time when he should be happily contemplating his own wedding he was trying to sort out the mess Ben had left even all these years after his death.

Once the serving of meals was finished and the pans washed the kitchen staff had time to spare before the last of the dirty crockery came down. It usually wasn't long but Betsy often stepped outside the door for a breath of fresh air. She did so this evening. She thought she had heard voices a few minutes before but no one came to the door and when she went out everything was quiet and peaceful.

She took several deep breaths and resolutely put thoughts of Daniel and the farm to the far recesses of her mind. It did no good to think of how it had been. For a long while she had hated Tom Shooter for what he had done, but she did so no longer. She didn't hate Daniel but she was disappointed because he had believed so easily what he thought he saw.

In her most generous moments she admitted to herself that it had looked bad. If it had been the other way round and there had been an undressed woman with Daniel in there would she have believed him to be innocent? In this ruthless mood she told herself she would not, so how could she have expected him to believe her? Especially with the 'evidence' that Tom Shooter had obviously planned so well. She had enjoyed more than three years of happiness and that was too good to last but at least she had the memory of it all and maybe one day...

She tried to shake off these thoughts and concentrate on her work as she opened the kitchen door to go back to her duties. Meanwhile Richard reached the end of the lane that took him to the stables where his horse was, and back at Redwood Farm Daniel sat down to a lonely meal of bread and cheese. Both men were thinking about Betsy.

Chapter 17

Two months had gone by since Betsy had left and Daniel could feel himself getting lower and lower in spirits. The work of the farm kept him going because he had to make a living and he had livestock depending on him. Yet as the weeks went by he grew more and more morose.

In the early days he had the hope that either she would return or he would find her, but now he had exhausted every avenue he could think of. The one thing he knew for sure in his heart was that she had not gone to Thomas Shooter. If only he had believed her in the first place, but it was far too late to dwell on what might have been.

Daniel had always faced facts but these were the toughest ever. He refused to think that he might never see her again because if he did that then his life truly would not be worth living. Betsy had brought a happiness beyond anything he had known and he dared to believe it had been the same for her, so he clung to the hope that he *would* find her and that she would want to come home to Redwood Farm with him. One evening he took down the straw halter and sat with it on his lap. Dumbo rubbed round his legs and he reached down and stroked the cat who looked at him with huge sad eyes.

'I know, Dumbo,' he said, swallowing hard, 'I miss her too. More than I could ever tell you.'

Later, in bed with Betsy's nightgown across his chest, he came to a decision. He would go and see Richard Choicely and tell him of Betsy's belief that he was her father. The man had after all taken more than a natural interest in Betsy, and in spite of Daniel's denials to his wife, he too was swayed by what Aunt Agnes had told her. He did not think she would have the power or imagination to make it up so it had to be the truth.

If, as Daniel thought, Betsy had sought work at the market and found a place, it was likely to be not a hundred miles away and Richard Choicely would have access to most of the families who employed servants. He could ask about any new staff they had taken on and they would tell him, whereas Daniel knew that alone he did not stand a chance.

He put his plan into action a few evenings later when he rode over to Chasebury Manor. Without going to find out, the butler said that Sir Richard was busy and could not see anyone. Daniel had deliberately shown up at Chasebury without an appointment because he had feared that this might happen. With a determination born of despair he told the butler that it was urgent and he only needed ten minutes of Sir Richard's time. 'Tell him it is Daniel Forrester of Redwood Farm, please. Sir Richard knows me.'

The unsmiling butler returned to say that Sir Richard Choicely would see Mr Forrester.

Richard offered him a drink. 'I have no news of your wife,' he said quietly, 'or have you come to give me news?'

'Not news, Sir Richard. I have none to tell. I do not know where my wife is. We had a misunderstanding over someone who worked for us. I lost my temper and she left. I have been trying to find her ever since.'

'I told you I saw her at the fair.'

'Yes. But she did not return and I have had no word from her.' He lifted his tankard to his mouth and drank before he said, 'When Betsy's mother died last year her aunt told her she had a different father from her brothers and sisters.'

Pausing, he looked to see what effect this was having on the other man, but Richard was studying his visitor calmly.

Daniel continued in a low voice, 'She told her she was the daughter of Sir Benjamin Choicely's son.'

The room was quiet as the men looked at

263

each other. Richard said, 'This was last year, you say. So that is not the reason she has gone missing?'

'Not the reason, no, but she wanted to find out if it was true. She became a little obsessed with the thought,' he kept his eyes fixed on his hosts face, 'and she might have sought you out for work after she left. It is my last hope, Sir Richard that she might have come here.'

'No, I have not seen Mistress Forrester since that day at the fair. I would have informed you. We agreed that, if you remember.'

Daniel shifted his gaze from the other man's face, 'Yes I know. I'm sorry. I do not doubt your word Sir Richard. I am worried for her safety, you understand, and am following up every lead I have. Thank you for seeing me. Good day, sir.'

He rose and Richard said, 'Please sit down again, Mr Forrester, and let us talk about your wife being my brother's daughter.'

'Your – brother's daughter?' Daniel could not keep the surprise out of his voice.

'Yes. Did you not know I had a brother?' Without waiting for a reply Richard went on talking. 'Ben was years older than me and the story you have been told is *possibly* true. I myself am trying to find out because there is a great family likeness on the maternal side.'

Looking at the stunned expression on his

guest's face he added, 'You thought it was me?'

When Daniel did not answer he said, 'Come, let me show you a portrait of my mother.' He led the way to the gallery and stopped in front of the painting. 'My mother when she was twenty-one,' he said.

Daniel gasped aloud. It could have been Betsy now.

'My brother died before Betsy was born. A riding accident.'

Daniel found his voice again. 'I'm sorry.'

Richard indicated another portrait a little further on. 'This is Ben when he was sixteen. As you see, he took after the maternal side of our family for looks.'

As they walked back from the gallery he said, 'But none of this is helping to find Betsy now, is it? Or indeed proving she is my brother's child, although from all I have learned lately I believe she is.'

When he left an hour later Daniel knew he had a powerful friend in Sir Richard Choicely, who promised to ask about new kitchen staff taken on in many of the large homes of the district and beyond. He was still inwardly reeling from the revelation that there was an elder brother who, Sir Richard admitted, had been irresponsible and a rogue. Betsy's likeness to Lady Choicely was remarkable, and her likeness to Benjamin Choicely, although not as marked because of hair and clothes and gender, was enough to convince Daniel that Aunt Agnes had told the truth about this.

He dared to hope that he would soon have news of Betsy. 'If only I knew where she was, Dumbo,' he said to the cat, as he stroked the animal's sleek black coat that evening. 'I love her beyond everything else in this world.' He went to the bookshelf and took down the Bible. The image of Betsy reading aloud from it was vibrant in his mind.

It would soon be time for another fair and Daniel was tempted to send Jim with the animals for sale, yet there was always the chance that he would find Betsy again simply by being there.

He recalled so clearly the first time he had set eyes on her, standing in a line with the others. He had been drawn to her immediately, although he had moved on and pretended to be interested in someone else. He had not gone to the fair with the intention of buying a wife. He had gone to sell some of his livestock and had wandered over to that section by accident when his business with the cattle was concluded.

He had not taken a wife before but when he saw Betsy the idea was born and from the moment he joined the men who were looking he knew she was the one he wanted. He looked at and briefly talked to others to suggest the idea that he was serious about this business. The truth was that once he had seen her it was as though he had been led to this section purposely. He longed, right from the start, to pick her up and carry her off, and when, just before he returned to ask her more questions, someone else was hovering he was petrified that he had missed his chance. When she answered him back he knew he had found a good one. He was captivated – a woman with such spirit and such beauty.

He was ashamed of his behaviour in the cart returning to Redwood Farm. He hadn't had a woman for some while and his basest instincts took over. Yet within hours he loved her for the woman she was and knew he would never want anybody else. The straw halter was his safeguard that no one could take her; she was his and he adored her.

Yes, he would go to the fair himself. If she wasn't there he might get word of her in the gossip that abounded at these gatherings. He had to find her again – he loved her more than he had ever loved anything or anyone in his life. Daniel began to make his preparations for the fair.

Agnes, now determined to pretend to Richard Choicely that she was Betsy's true mother and that her sister had only pretended to be so, trailed after him all over the fair.

I'll make him pay for his brother's sins, she said to herself. No one treats me like Ben did and gets away with it for ever. Ben didn't escape and neither will any member of that family. I've waited a long time for this but I'll have some of their money and bring that little madam down too. It is my right. He belonged to me before that thieving sister of mine got her filthy hands on him and had his child.

Agnes was a woman obsessed now with the grievance she had held inside through long years when she couldn't do anything about it. Each time she had seen Betsy, looking so like Ben and his mother, she felt they were stamping on her again, even from their graves.

So engrossed was she with her thoughts of revenge that she almost bumped into Daniel as he walked through the fairground looking to right and left in the hope of seeing his beloved wife.

'Ah,' she said, stopping him in his tracks, 'You've not found her then. But I have, and you can tell Sir Richard that. I want half whatever she gets to keep her mouth shut about who her father was. Tell him that too.'

Suddenly remembering her plan to say she was the mother, to add weight to her claim, she added sharply, 'He's marrying soon. His fiancée wouldn't like the nasty stories I have to tell about his brother and the mother of his child I'm sure. Well, my lips will be sealed – for a price.'

She poked him in the chest. 'I know you've seen him and he'll listen to you. Get the money for me and I'll take you to her.'

Realizing that Richard, her quarry, was out of sight she muttered something and strode off, pushing her way through the throng.

Daniel ran after her and clutched at her skirt. 'Just tell me where she is,' but she shook his arm away and was gone. He followed but although he tried to keep her in sight, within seconds she was lost to him, swallowed up in the laughing and noisy crowd.

Distraught, and not sure whether to believe Agnes he continued through the fair. It seemed as though everyone was here except the one he longed for. He had already been round by the cattle and worked his way through all the areas he thought might interest Betsy.

If Agnes really did know where she was, and deep in his heart he doubted it, but *if* she did, then he would get it out of her if he had to camp on her doorstep day and night.

Richard had come to the fair with his agent simply to do business and had not brought Lily with him. His plan was to go on to Clover Court when he left, to have a meal with the Aston-Jenkins family and spend the evening there.

His business done he found himself wondering whether Betsy Forrester would be here. Possibly only if she were looking for work, he thought. If she had employment and somewhere to live he doubted that she would come.

He did catch a glimpse of Daniel once, but before he could go through and speak to him the crowds closed in and he was lost to view. He liked the farmer and genuinely felt for him. He was kindly and, from what he could make out, he ran a good farm. Certainly he had a most beautiful wife, except of course that he didn't have her any more because she was missing.

Even so, she is still Daniel's wife and almost certainly my niece, he thought. So many searching yet not finding her. He pondered on the reason for her absence and was sure he had not been told the whole story. A misunderstanding, the farmer had said. Forcing his thoughts to his own affairs he tried to picture his fiancée, but a dark-haired beauty with amazingly deep-blue eyes and a sort of bloom on her features, intruded, jostling for his attention and blocking out the image of his own beautiful and fair Lily.

A deep sigh whispered throughout his being and Richard did not know whether it was a desire for Betsy the farmer's wife, or a yearning for the Beaumont family enchantment, which she had inherited and he had not.

Chapter 18

The next three-day fair Rosa and Bill were making for was in Applegate, on the borders of Sussex and Kent and just a few miles from Clover Court. As usual they travelled overnight and were well within the area the day before the fair began. Rosa walked along the lanes until she came to the back entrance of Clover Court, as before, and although she did not see Betsy she left word with Marie, the other kitchen-maid there, that she and Bill would be at the fair for two or three days, in the usual place and were looking forward to seeing Betsy.

'We are going in one day – cook told us, but I don't know which,' Marie said, 'I'll tell her you will be there. I won't forget, honest.'

Rosa felt such relief that Betsy was still working at Clover Court and would have the opportunity to go to the fair. In her prayers she asked with fervour for Daniel to be there too.

Bill said, 'Reckon he will be my Rosa, 'tis

a big fair and market and all the farmers'll attend.'

'But maybe not on the same day. Betsy will only be able to come once.'

'If 'tis meant to be it'll happen. If not and we see her Daniel we can point his trap the right way, then 'twill be up to them two.'

Rosa hugged him. 'Thought you said we shouldn't meddle, Bill.'

'We won't be meddling. I've thought about what you said though, and no harm to telling him what a nice place Clover Court is. And how far it is from the fair,' he added, smiling fondly at her.

They were at the site early as usual and had the caravan in place at the back on the edge of the woods long before the fair was declared open. They sat on the steps of the van watching the others roll in. Then they went off to find work with the cattle. All the while they were with the animals Rosa was watching for Daniel and Betsy. She saw neither of them.

Daniel went alone to the fair on the first day, leaving Jim in charge at the farm. He told his farm-hand they would go together the following day for the buying and selling.

'I have other business at the fair this day,' he said, as he handed Jim a bundle of food for him to eat during the time he was away.

Daniel went to the hiring-section first,

even though he knew Betsy would only stand in that line as a last resort. But if she was looking for work, and as far as he knew she had no money and would certainly have to find employment, that seemed the most likely place. He was concerned about how she was managing and torn between hoping she had already found a good place and wishing she would be at the fair looking for one.

There were many people there, from maids with mops to shepherds with crooks, each carrying the symbol of their craft while prospective employers walked along the line to talk to and select the workers they needed. Betsy was not among them.

Daniel moved on, past the stalls and booths where people were enjoying themselves after their business had been completed, and where there were many who came for the pleasures of the fair only. He paused by each food-stall, not to buy but to check whether Betsy was in charge. She was a good cook and he knew it would appeal to her to do this. If the women, hot from cooking sausages and pies, saw Daniel weave himself to the front of the crowd, round the stall and then work his way through to the back without buying, they had enough customers not to be bothered about one strange and worried-looking farmer.

Back in the body of the fair he scrutinized

each face as people jostled along, followed anyone ahead of him who had long dark tresses, until he was close enough to tell it wasn't the one person he was seeking. His emotions were on a see-saw as snatches of voices reached him, a laugh with an echo of Betsy's in it, a glimpse of someone the same sort of height and with a similar walk. Constantly he told himself what a fool he was to be roaming around like this when he should be working back at Redwood Farm, or buying and selling his stock here. Still that would be done tomorrow when he came in with Jim. Today he needed to look for Betsy. Life without her was bleak indeed. Even when they quarrelled, and he knew he had a stubborn temper, he also knew they would make up later in bed. When she let rip with her own volatile arguments, his excitement swelled until he thought he would burst. She stimulated him physically and intellectually, and without her now he felt only half-alive. Before Betsy, his farm and animals, with the occasional woman, had been enough. Since she had left, nothing but his beloved would ever be enough again. He wanted and needed nobody else.

Betsy had decided to turn down her chance to go to the fair in case she saw Daniel. She was still his wife and he would have the power to sell her. All her instincts told her he would *not* do this, but the image of his grim face as she had glimpsed him through the window holding the straw halter was strong.

There was also the prospect of bumping into Richard Choicely again and when he found out who she was working for he would think it strange, especially as she had run from him when he spoke to her about Daniel at the last fair.

When Marie told her that her friend Rosa had called and would be at the fair, she knew that she would go after all. In the short while she had known Rosa and Bill she had grown fond of them both and Rosa understood her as few others did. It would be good to be with them again for a few hours. She was afraid to hope too much that Daniel would be there, and if he was and she saw him she could not bear to think what she would do. She found herself longing for a glimpse of his beloved face, yearning to feel his hands caressing her again, yet she knew she would not approach him for fear of the consequences. It was hard to push the memories of Redwood Farm away, when she missed it all so very much, but whenever the memories threatened to overwhelm her she forced herself to picture in her mind the hated straw halter and Daniel taking it from the hook on the day she returned from trying to trace the boy called Zac. She had proved she could survive on her own and today she would be with her friends in their caravan most of the time so the danger of bumping into either Daniel or Richard Choicely was not great.

Betsy, Marie and one of the gardener's lads travelled to the fair in the cart driven by the under-gardener. The lad was cheeky with the two of them at first, happy to be on a fun day off, and Marie enjoyed his attention. Betsy was glad about this because she thought they might go off together and leave her free. Marie chatted excitedly for most of the journey and responded to the young boy's flirting while Betsy smiled in response but was quiet and thoughtful.

At least she had no need to look for work this time and could simply enjoy seeing Rosa and Bill again. She recalled to herself the first time she met them, at the fair where, if she had stayed at Redwood Farm, Daniel was going to sell her, and she shivered. He had been to that one. She remembered how she had lost her employment there because she ran off to avoid him seeing her. The pain she felt now seemed to flow all over her body. The ache in her heart reached new heights of sharpness as the cart bumped along the track. Soon they would be at the fair and she admitted to herself how much she longed to have a glimpse of him.

'Cheer up, Betsy. It's going to be such fun.' Betsy turned sharply as Marie poked her side and laughed. 'You look as if you're off to a fun'ral 'stead of a fair. Put a smile on with your clothes, my gran always says. Come on, there's lots to do and see and we can all stick together.'

'I'm meeting my friends, you remember, the lady who brought the message,' she said.

'Oh yes, 'course I do. Well...' Marie turned her head to one side and looked at the gardener's boy and Betsy breathed a happy sigh because she had been afraid that Marie would want to stay with her as there were only the two maids on the trip today. She was glad now that the gardening-lad was with them. It was clear she would have no bother there and on her return Marie would have lots to tell the girls she shared a room with.

When she left them, with instructions from the undergardener about the time they all had to be back at the stable-yard, she walked purposefully past the stalls and amusements, intent only on reaching the edge of the field where Rosa and Bill's caravan would be.

At the end of their first working stint Rosa and Bill wandered round as usual, pausing to look at stalls which interested them before returning to the caravan to see if Betsy had arrived. She was sitting on the grass at the side and she and Rosa fell into each other's arms.

'Come inside, oh, it is good to see you again.' Rosa said, 'how did you get here?'

'In the cart with Marie, one of the other maids, the one who started at Clover Court same time as me, the gardener's boy and the under-gardener.'

'It seems a good place where you are,' Bill said.

'It is but I'm going to move on soon if I can.'

'Why?' Rosa handed her a cool drink made from berries and herbs, and offered a plate of home-baked cakes.

Betsy took one and smiled her thanks. 'Because Lily, the daughter of the people I work for, is getting wed in the spring and I shall have to serve upstairs for the wedding and for some of the parties they are holding in the weeks before. The man she is marrying will recognize me, Rosa, and he will tell Daniel where I am.'

'Isn't that what you want, Betsy?' Rosa's voice was softly persuasive.

She could not pretend to Rosa.

'More than anything else, but I can't go back. He will try to bring me to market.' Two bright spots of colour flushed her cheeks as an image of Daniel with the straw halter in his hand flashed yet again into her mind. Her eyes bright with unshed tears she said, 'I won't risk it. You don't know how strong Daniel is over some things.'

They left her there when they returned to work, promising to go round the stalls with her when they finished their next session. 'It is so good to see you again,' Rosa said. 'How long can you stay?'

'All day. We left food for the family, and cook and two of the maids are going to be there. The rest of us will do it tomorrow when they come in.'

Less than ten minutes later, as they neared the cattle-market, they saw Daniel. Rosa went up to him and impulsively clasped his hand.

'It's Daniel Forrester, isn't it?' she said quickly. 'If you're looking for Betsy we left her in our caravan a short while ago.' She ignored Bill's warning look and went on, 'We are over at the far end where it's quiet. We'll show you if you like.'

Hardly daring to believe what she had said about Betsy he eagerly went with them.

Betsy sat for a few moments listening to the sounds of the fair in the distance. In her head she could hear Rosa's words about going back to Daniel. She would risk the humiliation of being turned away, she thought, because I walked out and I'll understand if he doesn't *want* me back, but much worse was the possibility of being sold again. No.

Never. She couldn't do that. It went against everything she had worked for, everything they had both worked for.

Reaching into the neckline of her dress she caressed the gold locket that Daniel had bought her. It was her most precious possession and she derived a deal of comfort from feeling it close to her skin.

She heard the sound of horses and looking towards the woods glimpsed the animals being tethered to a tree. Before she could scramble to her feet and get inside two rough-looking men appeared on the grassy patch by the side of the van. Unshaven and dishevelled, she could smell the ale on their breath as they pulled her up. One plunged his hand into the neck of her dress, ripping it open to reveal the locket, the other grabbed her hands shouting, 'Leave the bauble for now, we'll have *her* first, come on.'

As she struggled and tried to run towards the crowded fair, one of them slapped her hard across the face and spun her round towards the other, who did the same. Reeling from the blows and with her hands tightly gripped on either side of her, she was forced the opposite way into the woods.

She screamed and tried to drop to the ground so that she could crawl away but the two of them had her in such a strong grip that it was impossible. They dragged her along, but with the noise of the fair behind her, her screaming had no effect and they were getting further from the crowds with every second. Terrified, Betsy was panting with fear when suddenly they dived into a clump of trees.

If only one let go and she could aim a kick there was still a chance she could outrun them back to the fair. They were very drunk, so she might yet outwit them.

They all stumbled over a couple on the ground whose bodies were writhing and rolling together in agonized ecstasy, and with a loud oath one of the men fell on top of them. The other, still dragging Betsy with him, ran on. In vain she tried to wrestle her hand from his, she felt drunk with the fumes coming from his mouth as he cursed and swore and dragged her further into the wood.

As she screamed he put his free hand over her mouth and she bit into it as hard and deeply as she could manage. Blood poured from the wound as he danced around in agony but his good hand stayed imprisoning hers. Frantically she tried to free it but his hold was stronger than hers. Once again she did as she had done to Tom Shooter in the larder; she aimed a kick that forced her assailant to release her hand. Suddenly he was doubled up with pain and she was free.

She raced back through the wood towards the fair and straight into the arms of the other villain who had picked himself up and was heading towards her. For a moment or so they fought but he soon overpowered her and began ripping the clothes from her back even as he threw her, screaming, on to the ground, flinging himself heavily on top of her.

When Rosa, Bill and Daniel reached the van and saw the signs of a scuffle on the grass Bill said, 'The woods, you'd better stay here Rosa,' but she was already moving towards the trees where the horses were tethered.

Richard, walking over to the stable-yard where his horse was, spotted Daniel with two other people whom he did not know. He had completed his business at the fair and walked round the perimeter to reach the yard to avoid some of the crowds in the centre. At that moment screams rang out from within the woods. Daniel and his friends raced through the trees and without thought for anything except someone in trouble, he followed them.

As Rosa, Bill, Daniel and, a short distance behind, Richard, rushed through the woods towards the sound, Betsy's assailant was fighting what seemed to him like a mad-woman.

The other villain caught them up but before he could join in and help subdue the fiery Betsy who was flailing out with arms and legs, Richard, Daniel, Bill and Rosa burst through the trees. With four against them the two men soon ran off towards the horses, leapt on their backs and went thundering back through the woods and towards the fair.

Meanwhile Agnes, who had found and had been shadowing Richard Choicely for a while, saw him disappear through the trees behind the caravan. She panted along in his wake. It was now or never. She would *make* him listen and believe her and the future would be secure, no more scraping and bowing. She was sure he would listen when she threatened to tell his fiancée and her family about the child his brother had sired and how the Choicely family had treated her. Especially when she revealed that this offshoot was even now working for them. Oh yes, the revenge would be sweet for her.

She couldn't keep up with him, then she too heard the screams and stood still for a few moments to get her breath. The riders, galloping wildly back through the woods ploughed straight into her.

The accident at the fair which left Aunt Agnes dead shocked them all. None would have wished that kind of death on her, although Richard did see the justice of it more than most. An eye for an eye, he thought. He vowed to himself never to tell

Betsy the truth about his brother's death. It would do no harm to let her believe it was a real accident and not murder. The only person still alive now who knew the absolute truth was himself and he would take the secret to his grave.

The knowledge that Betsy had been working at Clover Court surprised both Richard and Daniel.

'Although,' Richard said to her much later when Agnes's body had been taken away and they were all sitting in Rosa and Bill's caravan, 'the person I saw near the stables that night looked familiar, I did not know it was you. For a moment I thought it was the ghost of my mother and wondered whether I had perhaps imbibed a little unwisely.'

Some time later, their arms wrapped round each other, Betsy and Daniel walked to the stable-yard and climbed into their farm-cart to return home. Before they left Richard Choicely said he was going to Clover Court from the fair and he would explain what had happened and why she would not be returning.

'Later,' he said, 'we must talk properly because you are part of my family, Betsy and,' he turned to Daniel, 'you also because she is your wife.'

'There is nothing I need,' Betsy said to him, her eyes shining and smiling in spite of the tragedy of a few hours ago. 'I only wanted to find the truth.'

Sir Richard bade them all farewell. 'Nevertheless, keep in touch,' he said.

Once clear of the fair Daniel reined in the cart and they kissed. 'My love,' he whispered tenderly, 'let's go home.'

An hour later, back at Redwood Farm Daniel stabled the horse then came into the room where she was making a fuss of Dumbo.

'Betsy, my dearest,' he whispered, taking her in his arms, 'I love you so.'

'And I love you, Daniel. I'll never leave you again. I was only half a person without you, my love.'

Suddenly he released her from his embrace. 'Wait, there's something I have to do, my darling, something I should have done a long time ago.' He took the straw halter from its hook in the kitchen, threw it into the grate and set light to it. As it crackled and burned he drew her once more into his arms, while the circlet of straw hissed and sparked before crumbling into ashes.

The publishers hope that this book has given you enjoyable reading. Large Print Books are especially designed to be as easy to see and hold as possible. If you wish a complete list of our books please ask at your local library or write directly to:

Magna Large Print Books
Magna House, Long Preston,
Skipton, North Yorkshire.
BD23 4ND

E. P.
Sheila
E. P.